"There's a tru⟨⟩ W9-AUS-713
It's been following us the whole time."

"I noticed," Jason said. "I saw it when we left town. Let's see what happens if we speed up."

The truck behind them accelerated as well, further closing the gap between them. Suddenly the truck slammed the rear bumper of their vehicle.

Danielle smashed against the door as Jason struggled to keep the car on the road.

"He's coming at us again."

With the truck still on their tail, Jason pumped the brakes and skidded off the road onto the widened shoulder. The truck flew past them as Jason's car came to a stop inches from the twenty-foot drop to the shoreline.

"You okay?" Jason asked.

"Besides the fact that my world has suddenly spun completely out of control? I guess I'm okay. What about you?"

"I'll live. Thankfully. If the driver's plan was to scare us, he succeeded."

What had just happened was clearly deliberate. Now all Danielle had to do was figure out how she was connected to a scam that had cost Garrett his life—and could have easily just cost them their own.

Books by Lisa Harris

Love Inspired Suspense

Final Deposit
Stolen Identity

LISA HARRIS

is a Christy Award finalist and the winner of the Best Inspirational Suspense Novel for 2011 from *RT Book Reviews*. She has more than twenty novels and novella collections in print. She and her family are missionaries in Africa, where she homeschools, works with women and runs a nonprofit organization called The ECHO Project, which "speaks up for those who cannot speak for themselves…the poor and helpless, and see that they get justice" (Proverbs 31:8, 9). When she's not working she loves hanging out with her family, cooking different ethnic dishes, photography and heading into the African bush on safari. For more information about her books and life in Africa visit her website at www.lisaharriswrites.com or her blog at http://myblogintheheartofafrica.blogspot.com.

STOLEN
IDENTITY

LISA
HARRIS

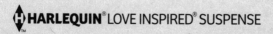

HARLEQUIN® LOVE INSPIRED® SUSPENSE

Recycling programs
for this product may
not exist in your area.

™ LOVE INSPIRED BOOKS

ISBN-13: 978-0-373-44542-4

STOLEN IDENTITY

Copyright © 2013 by Lisa Harris

www.LoveInspiredBooks.com

Printed in U.S.A.

Once you had no identity as a people; now you are God's people. Once you had received no mercy; now you have received God's mercy.

—*1 Peter* 2:10

To my three sweet children.
May you always find your identity in Him.

ONE

Jason Ryan snagged his cell phone from the kitchen table, then fumbled to answer before the caller hung up. The muscles in his jaw tightened as he checked the ID. Great. So the long lost prodigal had finally decided to check in.

He took the call, skipping any formalities with his best friend and business partner. "Where are you, Garrett?"

"Listen, I just have a minute. Some things have come up, and I…I need a few more days off."

"A few more days to do what?" Jason shoved the last file into his briefcase then slammed the lid shut. He didn't have time for more of Garrett's excuses. Not today.

"I can't tell you." His friend's voice faded in and out with the choppy connection.

"You can't or won't tell me? Come on, Garrett. I've put up with your excuses for weeks, and now you won't even answer my phone calls or respond to my emails. What am I supposed to do?"

"You don't understand—"

"No…" Jason let out a loud humph and started pacing the kitchen's mosaic tiled floor. "You're the one who doesn't understand, Garrett. I need you here. I just finished our final analysis of Simon's company and discovered another million dollars' worth of misappropriated funds. Do you realize how much work we have ahead of us?"

"I'm sorry, for everything, but I've gotten involved in something…something serious."

"Tell me what's wrong, and I'll help you fix it," he insisted, trying to reason with his friend.

"I don't think this can be fixed."

Jason rubbed the back of his neck. He could read the aggravation in his friend's voice, but he wasn't buying the excuses anymore. They might have become close friends over the past seven years, but even that didn't make up for Garrett's recent erratic behavior. Or the fact he'd been AWOL from his job the past two weeks. "Convince me why I shouldn't terminate you."

"Because I need you to trust me."

Jason frowned. As far as he was concerned, trust wasn't one of his friend's fortes at the moment. "It's a woman, isn't it?"

"Yes… No… It's not what you think."

Jason felt the last thread of patience snap. Garrett's record with women was worse than his own. While a fourth date always seemed one date too close to commitment for Jason, Garrett rarely got past a second date before he was playing the field again.

"Come on, Garrett…tell me what's going on." Jason rummaged through the kitchen cabinet for a bottle of aspirin to take the edge off the headache that had been brewing all morning. "Your mother called me yesterday, worried sick because she hadn't heard from you in over a week. Plus, I'm covering for you at work, even though I can't even tell anyone where you are or what you're doing because I don't know myself."

"Like I said, I can't tell you. Not yet, anyway."

"Then at least tell me where you are?"

There was a slight pause on the line. Jason downed the tablets with a glass of tap water. He set the empty glass in the sink, still awaiting an answer. "Garrett?"

"I'm in Pacific Cove, but nothing is secure…not on-line…not this call…."

Garrett's voice faded away.

"Garrett? Can you hear me?"

Even though the small coastal town was only twenty miles from his father's cabin, he hadn't been to Pacific Cove for years. What in the world was Garrett doing there?

"The connection is…bad." Garrett's voice returned. "I'll call you again in a few days. I've got to go."

"Garrett, wait—"

The line went dead.

Jason braced his hands against the sides of the kitchen sink and stared off into the distance at Mt. Hood shimmering in the morning sunlight. If Garrett was involved with a woman, why all the secrecy? Nothing made sense. He grabbed his car keys and briefcase and headed out the front door of his downtown Portland condo. Knowing Garrett, he was sitting at a beachside café eating crab cakes and oyster shooters with some girl he'd fallen for.

Some dire emergency. More like another one of Garrett's romantic liaisons. Or at least it had better be.

Four days later

Four-year-old Lauryn tugged on her mother's hand, her mouth drawn into a deep frown.

"What's wrong, sweetie?" Danielle Corbett followed her daughter's gaze past the foot-tall sandcastle wall they'd just finished. Another few minutes and the structure would completely disappear into the shoreline.

"Someone's out there."

Lauryn pointed to the swirling gray-blue waters of the Pacific Ocean dancing beneath the yellow sunlight that glistened off clusters of jagged rocks.

Something orange flashed in the water.

Danielle's gaze shifted to the right, and she squinted against the glare of the water. Another flash of color rose then disappeared. She scanned the deserted shoreline for help. Mr. Johnson walked his golden retriever most mornings. Reagan Garland jogged on the days he worked the night shift. Today, there was no one.

Grabbing Lauryn's hand, she ran toward her mother who had just finished gathering up their picnic supplies and handed her the beach bag. "Mom, there is a swimmer in distress. I need you to call 911 then take Lauryn with you up to the restaurant. Send someone for help, then wait for me there."

Not waiting for a response, Danielle hurried back into the surf, her tennis shoes soaking up the water and squishing beneath her sock-clad toes. Ignoring the Pacific Ocean's frigid temperature, she kept her focus on the figure as his head emerged gasping for air then vanished into the white foam.

A spray of water splashed her sun-chapped lips leaving behind its salty residue. Wiping the back of her hand against her mouth, Danielle trudged deeper into the ocean until she was only a few feet from the struggling body.

In an instant, he was gone.

Her toes barely touching the sandy bottom, Danielle searched the murky waters. Turning a full 360, her heart pounded frantically. Tufts of dark hair appeared at the surface. Diving into the water, she opened her eyes and aimed in the direction of the body. An eternity seemed to pass before the form appeared. This time he no longer struggled against the waves. An orange shirt hung off one shoulder. Heavy jeans hung like weights on his legs. Grabbing his shoulders, Danielle turned against the strengthening tide and headed for the surface.

Stay calm. Don't panic.

The emergency training course she'd taken last summer flashed before her. She took a deep breath and struggled to keep her head above the waves.

Pulling the man toward her, Danielle rested the back of his head against her chest. He lay limp in her arms. *Please God, don't let me be too late.* She checked the beach. It was empty.

One second at a time. One stroke at a time.

Pulling her free arm against the waves, Danielle pushed against the water until her feet touched the sand beneath her. The weight of the man grew heavy in her arms, but at least he wasn't fighting against her.

Danielle shivered, willing her body to keep swimming toward the shore, but even her training for this year's local triathlon hadn't prepared her for this. Underwater waves pushed against her legs. The sand sank beneath her feet making progress difficult. Ten more feet. She could see the edge of the water now. Five more feet.

Finally collapsing onto the wet sand, Danielle dragged the man far enough away from the incoming tide so that she could work unhindered. She looked to the deserted shoreline for help, worried that she didn't have time to wait for the paramedics to arrive, then gently shook his body. She felt for a pulse beneath his jawline and checked his breathing.

Nothing.

Danielle fought the alarm that rose in her chest as she placed the heel of her hand in the center of his chest and started chest compressions. A lock of dark hair rested against his forehead. Freckles scattered across his nose and cheeks. A small scar crossed his left eyebrow. He was somebody's son, brother, husband....

Lord, I need a miracle.

Danielle glanced up and drew out a labored sigh of relief at the man running toward her. Athletic build, dark blond hair... Pale blue eyes met hers a moment later as he knelt on the sand across from her.

"What happened?"

Danielle heard the urgency in his voice as she tried to catch her breath. Surely she was seeing things.

Jason Ryan?

His gaze shifted from her face, to the body, then back to her again. "Danielle? Tell me what happened," he said, his expression full of questions.

There was no time to process the familiar features...or the ten years that had passed since she'd last seen him. "I pulled him out of the water. I've tried CPR, but he doesn't have a pulse, and he's not breathing." Danielle felt her own heart pounding inside her chest. "My mother called 911 and has gone to the restaurant to get help."

He caught her gaze, then grabbed her hands, turning them over palms up. Danielle felt the air rush out of her lungs. They were covered with blood. "I don't think he drowned, Danielle. He's been shot."

Jason fought the panic as he tried to process the blood on Danielle's hands...and the fact that he'd just found Garrett. But if there was any chance of saving his friend, they both were going to have to keep their focus.

Needing to find the source of the injury, he turned his friend on to his side where the blood had seeped onto the sand. Two holes punctuated his back, leaving dark circles of blood behind. No pulse. No heartbeat. A sickening feeling flooded through him. Garrett was dead.

"We can still save him." Sirens wailed in the distance as Danielle knelt in front of Garrett's lifeless body and began the chest compressions again.

"It's too late." Jason grabbed her hands a second time and pulled them against his chest. "There isn't anything you could have done to save him. There isn't anything anyone can do. He's already gone, Danielle."

Already gone.

How had this happened? He stared at the lifeless body of his friend, then stood up, his legs shaking at the realization. His last conversation with Garrett raced through his mind as he walked a few paces toward the sea trying to process what had just occurred.

"Jason?"

"I knew him." He turned back toward her, guilt pounding through him. "I came to Pacific Cove to find him. He's a friend…my business partner."

"I'm so sorry." Danielle looked up at him with those achingly familiar, big brown eyes. "I can't imagine losing someone this way."

"I didn't take him seriously when he told me he was in trouble." Jason knelt back down onto the sand across from her. "Now he's dead."

Danielle stood twenty yards from the body—dead and lying in a body bag—she'd pulled from the ocean. The early afternoon tide swept back and forth across the rocky shoreline, sand flowers fluttered in the wind and seagulls fought for scraps of food beside her, but she barely saw any of it. Instead, her arms were crossed tightly against her chest as she answered the barrage of questions from one of the police officers, while another officer talked to

Jason. Where had she found the body? Had he been alive when she first saw him? Had there been any other witnesses at the scene?

Danielle shivered in the cold, trying to get her mind to focus, while absorbing the shock that a man was dead. Yes, she'd found him floating in the water. She thought he'd been alive when she pulled him out, but then they'd found the blood. There had been no heartbeat, no sign of breathing. And no, she hadn't seen anyone else on the beach at the time of the rescue except for Jason.

The officer tapped his pen against his notes. "One last question. Had you ever seen the victim before today?"

Danielle shook her head, wanting the interview to be over. Wishing she could erase the blank stare of the dead man's eyes looking back at her, the dark red stains on his back and the fact that her hands had been covered with his blood.

"Mrs. Corbett?"

"I'm sorry. No…I've never seen him before."

She barely heard the officer's instructions through her deafening thoughts. One of the officers would be in touch if they needed any more information. If she thought of anything else in the meantime, she needed to call the precinct. She gave him her contact information, then started walking away from the shoreline, wanting to get as far away as she could from the crime scene.

"Danielle?" Jason caught up to her. "Are you okay?"

"No, not really." Her clothes and shoes were soaked and she was shivering from the cold, but none of that seemed to matter. A man was dead.

"Do you need a ride home?"

She paused along the sandy trail leading toward the restaurant. She hadn't even stopped to think that far ahead.

"One of the paramedics let me use his phone to call my mom while he checked me out. I told her to take Lauryn home. If they were to see me soaking wet and shaken up like this, they'd both worry."

Besides that, the last thing she wanted was for either of them to have witnessed today's tragedy.

"Who's Lauryn?"

Danielle looked up into his turbulent blue eyes. She'd almost forgotten he didn't know. How much time had passed since the night she'd handed him her engagement ring back? Nine…ten years ago. It seemed like a lifetime. "A lot can change in ten years. Lauryn's my daughter."

"So you're married?"

She bent down and picked up a white sand dollar half-buried in the ground and started brushing off the sand. "Quinton died in a motorcycle accident two years ago."

"I'm sorry."

She let her thumb rub across the broken edge of the shell. Some days she felt the same way. Broken…defeated. Other days she felt as if she'd finally found her way. Today she wasn't sure where she stood. "It's something I'm learning to live with."

"Listen, let me go with you up to the restaurant so you can dry off and get something warm to drink, then I'll drive you home. You've got to be chilled to the bone. They have a fireplace in the dining room."

A shiver spread through her as he spoke, and she nodded. Late October meant the average temperature on the coast barely rose above sixty degrees. Being wet in the wind made the cold even worse.

She turned around to take one last look at the body before they headed toward the restaurant. Officers and paramedics finished working the scene, along with the medical examiner who had recently arrived. The reality of what had just transpired hit her like a winter storm beating against the Pacific's rugged coastline. When her knees buckled beneath her, Jason caught her and drew her into his arms.

She let him hold her for a moment. Her head rested against his chest as she breathed in the smell of salt and seaweed, finding an unexpected security in his presence. He had been that for her once. Years before she'd even met Quinton.

"I'm sorry." She stepped back, suddenly self-conscious of her display of emotion to a man she'd purposely forgotten. "I just don't think I've ever been so scared. Everything happened so fast.... I thought I could save him. I wanted so badly to save him."

"Hey, you don't have any reason to be sorry." He brushed away the tear sliding down her cheek with the back of his hand. "What you experienced today was traumatic."

Danielle looked up into his eyes again. The shadow of a beard covered his solid jawline, but despite his rugged looks, there was warmth in his expression. For a brief moment, memories of college and the Jason Ryan she used to know flashed before her. Weekends at the Saturday market sampling food and listening to music. Chinese takeout from Ling's. Day trips to the coast filled with fresh seafood....

She turned away from him, dismissing the memories. Whatever had been between her and Jason died years ago. But he was right about one thing. The situation had unnerved her. And she wasn't the only one.

Danielle shook her head. "I'm standing here, still in shock over the fact that I just pulled a dead body out of the water, but you knew him."

"I'm having a hard time believing that he's really gone."

They started up the path in silence until they reached the quaint seaside restaurant with its weathered shingle siding and 1920s architecture.

"Were you close?" she finally asked.

"We were friends. Good friends." Jason opened the side door to the restaurant, letting her slip into the warmth of the cozy great room with its thick, wooden ceiling beams and rustic decor. "We met a couple years after college and ended up starting an IT security company. Garrett and I have worked together ever since."

The name jarred Danielle's memory. She stopped in the doorway, breathing in the smell of fresh baked goods and seafood, and tried to dismiss the connection. No. The name couldn't be anything other than a crazy coincidence.

But what if she was wrong?

"What was his last name, Jason?"

"Garrett's last name? Peterson."

Garrett Peterson.

The room began to spin. He had called her. She'd thought he was nuts. And now he was dead.

"What's wrong, Danielle?"

"I'm not sure." She skirted a row of wooden tables and stopped in front of the stone fireplace, wondering how she'd just gotten thrust into a situation with both a murder victim and her ex-fiancé. She held her palms out toward the flame, wishing the warmth of the fire could somehow ease the numbness of the situation. "This has to be some uncanny coincidence, but I think your friend called me."

"Garrett?"

"Two days ago." Danielle locked eyes with Jason. This time it wasn't just her wet clothes sending chills down her spine. Somehow, Garrett's death was linked to her.

"Two days ago, I received a call from a man who told me his name was Garrett Peterson. He said his life had been ruined by a finance scam…and I was next."

TWO

Jason stood next to Danielle in front of the crackling fire, trying to wrap his mind around what she had just told him. Garrett had implied she was next…and now Garrett was dead. Jason turned toward her, trying to read her expression, and caught the fear and confusion in her eyes as she stared into the yellow flames. No matter what stood between them from their past, knowing her life could be in danger had invoked his protective instincts toward her.

Every plausible scenario he'd grappled with over the past few weeks had just been shot down. Finding Garrett dead was one scenario he'd never imagined. And he couldn't…wouldn't…let the same thing happen to her. Which brought him back to one probing question. How could Garrett have gotten himself tangled up with a financial scam, and how was Danielle involved?

"I don't understand." He tugged on the collar of his shirt. The room felt warm. Too warm. He took a step back from the fireplace, her nearness wreaking havoc with his equilibrium. "If Garrett had gotten caught up in some con, he would have told me. We were business partners, but more than that we were friends."

"I don't know. I didn't know him, or what he was involved in." She sat down at the table closest to the hearth, her back toward the flames. "All I know is what he told me. At the time I thought the call was some sort of prank and dismissed it as that, but clearly that isn't the case."

Jason slid into the seat across from her, still trying to fit the pieces together. Garrett had told Danielle that his life had been ruined by a financial scam. If Garrett knew Danielle was in danger, he must have found whoever had conned him and was trying to stop them. And warn her.

"Can I get the two of you anything?"

Jason glanced up at the waitress standing in front of them with a pen, a pad and a too-perky smile.

"Two coffees, please." He ordered for both of them automatically. "One black and the other with extra cream."

Jason turned back to Danielle as the waitress spun around to walk away. He rubbed his temples with his thumb and forefinger. Poignant memories of the two of them together had only managed to add to his own internal turmoil. How many times had he ordered for both of them at some quaint, corner café? Stared into those same familiar brown eyes. But that was a lifetime ago. He shouldn't assume that she—or her tastes—had stayed the same. "I'm sorry. I should have asked you what you wanted. If you'd like to order something else—"

"No. Coffee—with extra cream—is fine." Her knowing gaze seemed to reverberate right through him. "Italy expanded my taste buds a bit when it comes to coffee, but I'm impressed you remembered."

"You were right. A lot has changed." He quirked a brow. "So what *are* your coffee drinking preferences these days?"

She shot him a smile. "Sitting outside a café in Rome or Venice sipping an espresso."

He couldn't help but grin back. She'd changed little besides a few extra smile lines, and her cinnamon-brown, shoulder-length hair had turned a shade or two darker. He'd pictured her from time to time, wondering where she was and what had happened to her, but he'd never tried to find her. Somehow, the distance between them had made it easier for him to forget. Because Danielle had been the first woman he'd ever really loved. And if he was honest, the last.

But he had no intention of having his heart broken again.

Jason shook his head and shoved the past back where their relationship belonged. He might not be able to deny that he was still powerfully drawn to her, but there were simply too many things that had to be figured out right now. "Let's go over what happened. You said Garrett called two days ago?"

"Monday evening. I'd just gotten home after picking up Lauryn from my mom's."

"What exactly did he say?"

Her chin quivered slightly as she answered. "He... he told me that his name was Garrett Peterson, then he started rambling about how his life was in shambles, and how I was going to be next. He was scared, Jason. I could hear the fear in his voice."

The waitress set two thick mugs in front of them. Jason waited until she left, thankful it was off-season and there was only one other couple in the restaurant. At least here they had a measure of privacy. Over the years, he'd imagined what it might be like to be alone with her again. But not like this. Not under these circumstances.

He grabbed two packets of sugar from the container on the table, ripped them open then dumped the contents into his coffee. "What did you tell him?"

"Nothing." Danielle added a packet of sugar then took a sip before setting the mug back on the table. "I hung up on him. I honestly thought he was crazy or had the wrong number. But now…I realize he had to have been trying to tell me to watch my back."

Jason tried to work through the timeline of the past few days. On Saturday, Garrett had called asking for more time off, which now seemed to imply he'd been looking for something, or someone. When he called Danielle on Monday, he'd sounded afraid. He'd lost everything financially and somehow the situation was connected to Danielle. Now he was dead. The situation was beginning to read like some horrible, low-budget movie script.

"You knew him." Danielle ran her long, delicate fingers across the handle of the mug. "Had he been acting strange lately?

"A couple months ago, I started noticing some subtle changes in him. I chalked it up to the death of his grandfather. You know what happens when someone close to you dies—it can make you reevaluate your own life. That's what I thought happened to Garrett. He started taking vitamins, working out more at the gym, even cut out sugar and fast food. But he also seemed preoccupied and distant."

"Some kind of early midlife crisis?" she asked, her wide brown eyes flickering with interest.

"That's a good name for it. But no matter how many times I tried talking to him, he always told me not to worry, that everything was fine."

"Could he have brought this on himself? What about gambling?"

He shook his head. "I don't think so. He wasn't the addictive type, nor can I imagine him throwing away everything we've worked so hard for over the past few years. He'd even invested recently in a new house."

"So he never talked to you about financial problems."

"If he had any, I didn't know about it. I actually assumed he was doing fine. He helped out his sister's family while his brother-in-law was out of work, and always gave generously to his church." He sighed. "Whatever financial issues he was facing—whatever they might have been—he kept them to himself."

Jason added another packet of sugar, restirred his coffee, then set down the spoon, wanting to dismiss the assumption. "What I don't understand is how does a security expert fall victim to a con? Garrett's job was to ensure companies were protected from online threats. More than anyone, he knew how to protect himself."

"Think about it." Danielle didn't look convinced. "How does anyone get involved in these kinds of scams in the first place? It's never intentional. I read the news enough to know that identity theft is on the rise, and all it takes is one mistake by the victim that leaves them vulnerable. What I don't understand is the connection to me."

"Identity theft is usually random."

"Which would imply that it's also a crime of opportunity."

"What about you?" He took another sip of his coffee. Somehow, they needed to find the connection between Danielle, Garrett and their scam artist. "Are you still involved in archaeology and history?"

"When Lauryn was born, I decided to give up my career so I didn't have to travel so much. Now I own a small shop in town called The Bamboo Closet. It's an eclectic collection of home decor, furniture and gifts sold primarily to tourists."

Her profile fit. While random, thieves would want to target people with assets.

"So how could someone get to you?" Jason started throwing out ideas "Do you shred all your documents before throwing them away?"

Her left brow quirked. "Yes."

"What about any missing credit cards?"

"None."

"A stolen wallet or any missing bills?"

She shook her head. "Nothing and my mailbox has a lock, so I can be pretty sure that no one has been in it."

Jason paused with his line of questions. She was looking to him for answers. He was trying to deal with the situation as if she were simply another client needing his expertise. But trying to convince himself that this wasn't personal wasn't working.

"I suppose there is no way to know at this point how this happened," he continued. "Someone could have hacked into the computer of one of your credit card companies, or bribed a county clerk for your personal information for that matter. The real question seems to be how did Garrett know that you'd be next?"

"I don't know." Fear registered in her eyes. "But I can't let the same thing happen to me. I have a daughter, a business… If Garrett was right, I could lose my shop, my house…everything I've worked for over the past few years."

He reached out and squeezed her hand. "We're not going to let this situation get that far."

"We?" Her voice caught, but she didn't pull away from his grasp.

"You need to make sure that what happened to Garret doesn't happen to you…and I not only need answers to my friend's death, but reassurances that the security of my company hasn't been compromised." Tightening his grip on her hand, he gave her a reassuring look. "No matter what happened between us in the past, Danielle, we're in this together."

Ten minutes later, Danielle pressed her fingers against the armrest of Jason's car as he followed the coastal road running parallel to the shoreline. Even after seven years of living here, she'd yet to grow tired of the view from the windy highway perched above narrow coves and rocky cliffs below. With the added green forests and the unending ocean, Pacific Cove had become her personal safe haven.

Until now.

She glanced over at Jason, who'd said little since they'd left, and studied his face. His hair had darkened some since the last time she'd seen him, but the left dimple was still there when he smiled, along with his familiar wide, square jaw and pale blue eyes. The years between them had only seemed to add to his charm. That same charm had instantly captured her heart when she was a college freshman. Jason had been the life of the party, the one who could always make her laugh…the one who'd taught her how to take life less seriously.

"You never told me why." Jason's even tone broke into her thoughts. "Never told me why you broke off our engagement."

Danielle swallowed hard and turned back toward the window at the rush of unwanted memories. She'd known this subject would surface, but she wasn't ready to talk about the past. Not here. Not now. Not while trying to deal with a murder and the thought of her own life—and her daughter's—in danger.

"Our engagement was a long time ago." Nothing she

could say would change what happened…or lessen the tension presently hanging between them. "I made some foolish decisions out of fear. I knew you deserved more, but at the time I didn't know how to deal with everything I was feeling."

"What were you feeling?"

She fingered the sand dollar she'd dropped into her pocket, letting her thumb trace back and forth across its smooth ridges. Everyone had been shocked when, after graduating from college, she chose to join a three-year archaeological dig in Italy over marrying her college sweetheart. Even all these years later, she still carried regrets from that decision. Regrets of walking away without ever telling Jason the truth. Regrets of knowing she had broken his heart. Of wondering if she'd told him the truth would her life have turned out differently. But sometimes the past was better kept in the past.

She turned back to his strong, familiar profile and caught the hurt in his expression, bringing with it a fresh wave of regret. "I can't change what happened, except to say I'm sorry for hurting you."

She was avoiding his question, she knew that. He wasn't asking for an apology, but an explanation. But while Jason might not have been her father, back then she'd struggled to believe that Jason would turn out to be any different. And while she had loved him, in the end, she'd allowed fear to push him out of her life.

She shoved the thoughts from the past aside, hating the unease hovering between them. She was happy with her organized, predictable life, where one plus one always equaled two and there were never any bad guys waiting in the wings—or murder victims to pull out of the water. She'd become content with days spent running her shop, evenings and weekends with family and friends, church on Sundays, volunteering at the homeless shelter and days off with Lauryn sprinkled in as often as she could.

Today, though, nothing added up. Nothing felt familiar except perhaps the surfacing memories of feelings she'd once held for the man sitting beside her. Instead, she had no point of reference on how to react after finding a murdered body. Or what to do when one somehow became tied to a fraud victim. Dealing with the past only added to the complication. What she needed now was answers, and the only place she knew to find them was with Garrett Peterson.

"Where did you meet Garret?"

"A few years after college at a job fair." Jason kept his gaze on the road while he spoke, seeming to accept—at least for the moment—her changing the subject. "We were both unhappy with our current positions and decided we could do a better job running our own company. Eventually, we did."

"That had to have taken a lot of courage—starting your own business."

"There were moments when I was convinced I should have continued working for someone else, but five years later we're still in business, so I'd say hanging in there was a good move."

She glanced over at him. "You mentioned a security company?"

"Garrett had experience in computers security and cyber-research—simply put, he's a genius as an ethical hacker. I had a lot of financial business experience. Together, we were able to form a company that deals with issues like asset recovery, online security and even financial fraud investigations."

Danielle stared out the window at the passing shoreline down below as a picture came into focus. "Sounds like you both have done well for yourselves. What was he like?"

"Garrett? He was somewhat of a good ol' boy. Women thought he was funny and charming. Most men trusted and respected him, at least when he wanted to be taken seriously." Jason's fingers tightened around the steering wheel. "He has a sister, a brother-in-law and twin nieces born earlier this year. His parents still live in the same house where he grew up, and he still has a room there… though he moved out years ago. He was your ordinary computer geek who was great at his job, loved video games and movies, and had just enough independence—or maybe stubbornness—to where he never managed to find the right woman who would put up with him."

The dimple in his cheek was back, taking her places she didn't want to go. She shifted her gaze again to the window overlooking distant blue-gray waters. "What about you? Did you ever find the right woman?"

"Me?" Jason was quiet for a brief moment. "Once I thought I'd found her, but I realized I was wrong."

Danielle pressed her lips together, wishing she hadn't asked. There was no way to erase the years between them, nor were they years she wanted to erase. Even for the boy who used to bring her wildflowers and seashells, and who had once held the key to her heart.

"There is still one more question that has to be asked," she began, switching gears back to the investigation. "Why would someone have wanted to kill Garrett? How does a presumably cut-and-dried case of identity theft or financial fraud escalate into murder?"

He strummed his fingers against the steering wheel. "I don't know what the answers are. I don't know how he let himself be pulled into some scam, let alone why anyone would want to murder him."

Danielle waited for him to continue.

"I've gone over and over every phone call and conversation we've had lately," Jason finally said. "He'd been distracted for weeks. Missed a lot of work, but he wouldn't tell me what was going on even when I asked him straightout. I thought he'd met someone, but even if that were true, why all the secrecy?"

"So you think there could have been a woman involved in this?"

"It's possible. If Garrett did fall prey to some financial scam like he told you, maybe it's because he let his guard down and trusted the wrong person. Women often make the perfect diversions."

As she mulled that over, Danielle watched the distorted reflections of the forest fly by through the passenger-side mirror. Fear twisted through her. Whoever killed Garrett was after her. Something caught her attention in the mirror. The same black truck she'd noticed when they'd pulled out of the parking lot of the restaurant was still trailing behind them.

Danielle shivered, dismissing the thought they were being followed. With few places to turn off from town to her house, having a car behind them wasn't something to worry about. She was simply being paranoid.

She looked at Jason, wondering if he'd noticed. "There's a truck behind us. It's been following us the whole time."

"I noticed." He glanced up at the rearview mirror. "I saw it when we left town."

"This has to be a coincidence. It's not like there are a lot of places to pull off on this highway."

"Coincidence or not, my best friend is lying in the morgue after being shot twice in the back. I'd say a bit of paranoia is simply a precaution at this point." He pressed his foot against the accelerator as he took the next curve in the road. "Let's see what happens if we speed up."

The truck behind them accelerated, as well, further bridging the gap between them.

Danielle turned around, trying to get a better look at the driver. Dark clothes, cap pulled low, sunglasses… Nothing to identify him.

The truck sped up until he was right behind them. "Maybe he'll pass—"

"Hang on!" Jason interrupted. "He's not passing, and he's not slowing down—"

Suddenly, the truck slammed the rear bumper of their vehicle.

Danielle smashed against the door as Jason struggled to keep the car on the road.

"He's coming at us again."

Heart pounding, she braced herself against the door as Jason was forced to slow down in order to take the next curve. Their right tire dropped off the edge of the pavement, and the car skidded against the metal guardrail. "If he hits us again now, we'll go over the edge…."

Fifty feet ahead, the shoulder widened. If they could make it that far, they might be able to pull off and stop. Danielle held her breath and braced for a second impact.

Thirty feet… Fifteen…

With the truck still on their tail, Jason pumped the brakes and skidded off the road onto the widened shoulder. Gravel spewed from behind the back tires as the car started sliding toward the edge of the road.

The truck flew past them as Jason's car came to a stop inches from the twenty-foot drop-off above the shoreline. Danielle leaned back against the seat, struggling to breathe.

"You okay?"

She drew in a rugged breath, her hands shaking in her lap. "Beside the fact that my world has suddenly spun completely out of control, and I'll probably have a couple bruises in the morning? I guess I'm okay. What about you?"

"I'll live. Thankfully." Jason gripped the steering wheel. "There wasn't a license plate."

"I know. Dark clothes, hat pulled low. He didn't want to be seen."

"If his plan was to scare us, he succeeded."

What had just happened was clearly deliberate. Now all she had to do was figure out how she was connected to a scam that had cost Garrett his life—and could have easily just cost them their own.

THREE

Danielle stepped into the four-bedroom beach house she and Quinton had bought as an investment the year after Lauryn was born. Everything looked exactly the same as when she'd left this morning. Framed family photos lined the hand-carved wooden mantel, a pile of green apples sat in a wrought-iron bowl on the kitchen bar, the large mirror over the couch still hung a bit crooked. Even the stack of junk mail next to the door hadn't been touched. No sign that anything unusual had transpired this afternoon.

It was the same feeling she'd experienced when Quinton died. The day she'd walked back into her house after burying him, she'd been struck by the fact that everything was exactly the same. His toothbrush sat on the vanity beside their half-used tube of toothpaste. Socks and underwear lay scattered on the bathroom floor.

Nothing had changed, while at the same time everything had changed.

Lauryn ran into the living room wearing her favorite pink ballerina outfit and carrying her worn, stuffed Eeyore. Danielle gathered her daughter into her arms, breathing in the strawberry scent of her just-washed hair. And thankful for the sense of normality she brought. Still holding Lauryn against her, she turned to Jason who had just shut the door behind them.

"Jason, this is my daughter, Lauryn."

Jason knelt down and tugged gently on one of her pigtails. "It's nice to meet you, Pigtails."

Lauryn shook her head and giggled. "My name is Lauryn, not Pigtails."

"Aah…Lauryn, that's right. You have a beautiful name." He leaned forward and whispered in her ear, loud enough so they all could hear. "But I still like the name Pigtails."

Lauryn laughed again then snuggled against Danielle's legs.

"You always were a cutup, Mr. Ryan."

Danielle's mother, Maggie, strolled into the middle of the room sporting her newly ash-blond look with a pair of cropped pants and a matching, flowery top.

Jason shook her mother's hand. "It's good to see you again, Mrs. Taylor. I don't think you've changed a bit since the last time I saw you."

"You always were a charmer, too. Don't tell Danielle, but I was disappointed when she called off the wedding. You always could make me feel twenty-nine again. I miss that."

Danielle felt her jaw tense. "Mother, I'm standing right here."

"Well, what I said is true. Though, Jason, you are the last person I expected to show up in Pacific Cove after all these years. We lost track of you after graduation."

"Jason runs a security company in Portland." Danielle ran her fingers through Lauryn's pigtails, hoping to steer the conversation away from anything too personal. Like the last time she'd seen him.

"Sounds as if you've done quite well for yourself, and

what about your father?" Maggie asked. "I haven't seen him for...well at least a decade."

"He still lives north of here about twenty miles or so."

Her mother nodded. "It's hard to believe I haven't run into him after all these years. Did he ever remarry?"

"Actually, no. He seems content charming the women, without committing to anything."

"Like father, like son?"

Jason's gaze dropped. "If you're asking if I'm single, as well...the answer is yes."

"Mother." Danielle cleared her throat. It was time to change the direction of the conversation. "I'm sorry we took so long. It ended up taking a lot longer than I imagined."

"What happened down there? You had me all in a panic and you're a mess."

Danielle glanced down at her wrinkled clothes. This wasn't a conversation her daughter needed to hear.

"I bet you've got a great view of the ocean from up here," Jason said to Lauryn. "Do you think you could show it to me?"

Danielle mouthed *thank you,* then turned back to her mother as Lauryn skipped toward the patio door with Jason and Eeyore in tow.

Maggie leaned against the back of the couch. "You know I wouldn't have missed out on having Quinton for a son-in-law for anything, but I always liked Jason."

"He was...*is* a good guy. I just wasn't ready for marriage back then."

Her mother arched a brow. "This clearly isn't a happy reunion, though, is it? What happened?"

"The man I pulled out of the ocean died. Turns out he was Jason's friend and business partner."

She wasn't ready to tell her about the gunshot wounds,

or the fact that they'd almost been run off the road. The police had promised to be on the lookout for the vehicle, but hadn't offered a lot of reassurances that they'd find the driver. She reached up and touched the bruised shoulder she'd slammed against the car door. There were too many unanswered questions, and her mother would only worry like she always did.

"Are you okay?"

"I've had better days," Danielle admitted.

Her mother frowned. "I had plans to go out with a few friends tonight for dinner, but I'm not sure I want to leave you here alone."

"I'm fine, Mother."

She looked uncertain. "How can you say you're fine after pulling a dead body out of the Pacific. I'd really feel better if you let me just stay here and fix you some homemade soup…."

"You don't need to worry…I promise." Danielle opened the entryway closet, grabbed her mother's coat and handed it to her. "You go have a good time with your friends."

The last thing she needed right now was the probing questions of her well-meaning mother.

With a sigh, Maggie gathered up her purse and slung it over her shoulder. "All right…if you insist. But I'll call when I get home tonight and make sure you're okay."

A moment later, Danielle shut the door behind her mother then leaned back against it as Jason and Lauryn came back inside with the little girl's hand tucked tightly into his.

"Can he stay for dinner, Mommy?"

Jason pulled his keys out of his pocket. "I'd love to, Pigtails, but I have some things I have to do tonight—"

"Wait." Danielle hesitated, knowing she shouldn't ask

him to stay. "You could stay for a while. You could call Garrett's parents from here and help me figure out where to start. That is, if you don't mind."

Jason cocked his head. "I don't mind at all, but are you sure?"

Danielle nodded. The truth was that while she wanted to avoid her mother's probing questions, the last thing she wanted was to be alone right now. "I can whip up a box of macaroni and cheese later if you're hungry."

Lauryn squealed with delight.

"That just might cinch the deal." Jason grinned. "I do love mac and cheese."

Danielle looked down at Lauryn and smiled, intent that her daughter wouldn't sense what was really going on. "Sweetie, Jason and I need to talk for a few minutes before dinner. Why don't you take Eeyore and have a tea party with your stuffed animals. You can even have a few gingerbread cookies from the cabinet, if you'd like."

A moment later, Lauryn was skipping down the hallway with her treats in hand. Danielle turned back to Jason, wishing she didn't feel so vulnerable.

"You really don't mind staying, do you?"

There was a long pause. "I don't think I want to be alone right now any more than you do," he admitted.

"Good, because I meant what I said. I don't even know where to start." Danielle swallowed hard. She'd been through worse. The death of her husband, struggling as a single mom, running a business on her own. She would get through this. As long as she could figure out what exactly she was up against.

"First, you'll need to go online and access all your accounts—credit cards and banking—to see if there is any sign of fraudulent activity. And I guess I have a phone call to make."

He was dreading calling Garrett's parents. She could see the worry in his eyes. Just like she was in no hurry to face the computer, afraid of what she might very well find when she went through her accounts.

"Do you know Garrett's parents well?"

"I spent a lot of holidays there. Mrs. Peterson was an incredible cook. Christmas roast turkey and homemade stuffing, New Year's black-eyed peas—"

"Whoa." She folded her arms across her chest and shook her head. "You're making me feel a bit insecure about my boxed mac and cheese."

"Don't be." Jason laughed. "Remember, I'm the guy who used to live on ramen noodles and Cap'n Crunch. I survived that, didn't I?"

She did remember. Too much. His love for classic cars, shooting ranges, French fries dipped in honey and scrambled eggs with ketchup….

"Why don't you make that phone call, and as soon as I've had a quick shower and change of clothes, I'll start searching online."

Fifteen minutes later, Danielle sat down at her computer in the corner of the living room and clicked on her internet browser. She thought she'd always been so careful. Never using public computers, never following links in emails claiming to be from her bank, never sending online banking credentials via text messages.

She glanced at Jason, who was still on the phone, his expression grim. He was the last person she'd expected to walk back into her life, but despite everything that had happened between them, there was something comforting about having him here.

He hung up the phone, then crossed the room. "Anything?"

"Nothing yet, but I have a feeling it will take a while

to go through everything." She tried to read his expression. "What about Garrett's parents?"

"I decided that rather than tell them over the phone, I needed to contact their pastor. He's driving over there right now. I also spoke with Mandy, Garrett's sister. She's in shock, but is planning to meet Pastor Mike at her parents' house." He scrubbed a hand across his face. "The police promised to keep his name from the media until the next of kin was told, but it's going to take some time for them to let all of this sink in. They were a close family."

"I'm so sorry. I know how hard this is on you."

He turned away, but not before she saw the pain flickering in his eyes. "I'll drive up to their place in the next day or two. See if there is anything I can do to help.…"

Danielle suppressed the impulse to step into his arms and comfort him. Except she no longer held the key to his heart. "It will mean a lot to them for you to be around."

A new email popped up on her screen. Danielle clicked on the message automatically, started reading, then froze. "Jason, you need to take a look at this."

He leaned in closer, reading over her shoulder.

Your account is being held for ransom in exchange for the information obtained by Garrett Peterson. You have twenty-four hours. If you don't believe I'm capable of doing further damage—check your bank records.
Il Truffatore

Danielle gripped the mouse with her fingers. "Garrett was right."

She didn't know how, but he'd found her.

Jason scooted a chair over from the dining room table and sat down beside her. "*Il Truffatore?* What does that mean?"

"It's Italian. It means *The Swindler*."

"Skip the credit card accounts for now and look at your bank records."

She clicked through her bank's website and entered her user ID and password. It didn't take long to find what she was looking for. Nausea spread through her as she read through the statement. "Six days ago, there was a $350,000 transfer from my home equity loan." She couldn't breathe. "I never authorized this, Jason."

"He expected to be long gone before you ever found out about it."

She gazed at him in confusion. "I don't understand. How did he do this?"

"I'm not sure, but there is a good chance that the money has already been transferred out of the country."

"He'll ruin my credit, and I'll lose my business."

"Not if we can stop him," he fired back.

"What about IP addresses?" Danielle searched for something, anything that would help them figure out what was going on. "Can't someone's location be traced that way?"

"Typically yes, but someone like him will know how to hide his tracks. Still, it's worth a try. Scoot over for a second." Jason leaned over and started typing on the keyboard.

Danielle felt the panic set in. If he was nearby and knew where she was…

"There he is…" A few minutes later he had the answer. "The IP address is from China."

"Meaning?"

"More than likely he's used a proxy server to change his IP address. We're not dealing with your run-of-the-mill hacker here. This guy clearly knows what he is doing."

Danielle shook her head. "It has to be the same man. The man who murdered Garrett. The man who just tried to kill us."

The man who just stole over a quarter of a million dollars from her.

"If he thinks we have—or have access to—something he wants, his plan must have been to scare us."

She pushed her chair back. "But what evidence does he want?"

"I don't know. If Garrett had been collecting evidence against this guy, then it makes sense that he could have also found out other people he was scamming."

"So Garrett had evidence to take this guy down and ended up confronting him?"

"Maybe." Jason grabbed his phone from his back pocket and punched in a phone number. "I'll give the police an update, but with their limited time and resources, I also want to call one of our tech guys. If anyone can find this guy, Philip can."

Danielle listened to Lauryn singing Disney songs from her bedroom. She closed her eyes and pictured her sitting at her little wooden table, having tea with Sam, Buddy and Eeyore. She couldn't let this touch her daughter.

"I'll forward the email now." Jason's voice broke into her thoughts as he spoke into the phone. "The IP address is hidden, but see what you can do to track down the source. And there's something else I'm worried about. The more I process this situation, the more I'm concerned that Garrett could have been involved in something that has compromised our own security. I'm going to need you to put together a team, because this guy clearly knows what he's doing...."

Danielle got up and walked to the back patio, needing some fresh air. The brilliant orange sun cast streaks of light across the dark blue Pacific. She shivered in the cold breeze wishing there was something she could do to make what had happened today disappear.

Waves crashed in the distance, as the sun sank below the horizon. She'd wrestled with fear before, but today's panic threatened to completely overwhelm her.

I don't even know which way to turn, God. If I lose everything, I need to know that You are still there....

The back door opened and closed behind her. She turned around. Jason stood at the edge of the patio beneath the outside lamp that gave off just enough light to catch his gloomy expression.

"Philip is going to work with us to find this guy."

She leaned against the wooden rail behind her, studying the hard lines of his face and the tense set to his wide shoulders. Suppressed feelings of longing swept over her, causing her breath to catch. She turned back to the sea in an attempt to contain them. "From what I overheard, I'm not the only one facing loss."

"We have contracts with a number of companies who work with classified information. A breach in our security could be devastating."

"So you'll be going back to Portland?" she asked.

"For now I feel like it's better I stay here. Philip is putting a team together, and we'll meet in the morning via a video conference."

She took a step toward him, hoping the relief she felt over the fact he was staying didn't show. She wasn't going to let her heart get involved this time around. But even the fact that he was staying wasn't enough to eradicate the fear.

"He ruined Garrett. You're looking at possible security compromises. I've got my shop and Lauryn to consider. I don't know how to play this game."

He stared into her eyes. "I promise, we're going to figure this out. Whatever it takes."

She still wasn't convinced there was a way to win. "Garrett tried on his own and look what happened to him. Whoever this guy is, he's smart. He knows what he is doing, and he's willing to kill to protect what he has." She looked up at him, wishing for a brief moment that he would wrap his arms around her again and make her feel safe. Even if it was only for a moment. "What if I can't keep Lauryn safe?"

What if Jason's promise wasn't enough? What if everything they did wasn't enough?

FOUR

Danielle pushed back one of the soft ringlets lying against Lauryn's neck then closed the book they'd been reading together. These quiet moments, the ones that hovered between hectic days of trying to balance the needs of a pre-schooler with running a business, had always been her favorite time. It wouldn't be too many years before tea parties, dress up and sandcastles on the beach were replaced with phone calls from boys and trips to the mall with friends. Which meant that for now, Danielle was content to savor these rituals for as long as they lasted.

Lauryn fought to keep her droopy eyes open. "Will you read one more chapter, Mommy?"

Danielle kissed Lauryn on the forehead, before setting the book on the wicker bedside table. "I think we've had enough for one night, sweetie."

Stress had brought on an achy tiredness that had spread through her body and left her mind in a fog, making even the simplest of tasks challenging. The land of Narnia, and all that was transpiring on the other side of the wardrobe, would have to wait until tomorrow night.

Lauryn's lips puckered into a frown. "I'm not tired."

"You're not tired?" Danielle straightened the collar of Lauryn's pink pajamas. "That is a problem, because

Grandma told me that since tomorrow is Wednesday, she's planning to take you to story time at the library. Would you like that?"

Lauryn yawned then nodded.

"Do you know what else that means?" she asked her daughter.

"That I get ice cream. Grandma always takes me out for ice cream after the library."

Danielle laughed. "What I meant was that you need to get some sleep."

She nuzzled her daughter's nose then finished lining up the row of stuffed animals sprawled out along the edge of the bed before standing up.

"Do you think he'll come back to see us?"

Danielle stopped in the doorway. "Jason?"

Lauryn nodded.

Danielle's mind fought to hold on to the slowly fading memories from the past. Memories she wasn't sure she was ready to let go. Quinton had loved tucking Lauryn in at night. Their bedtime ritual had consisted of bath time, story time and giggles until Danielle had to insist that morning would come all too soon if they didn't get to sleep.

And now Jason had somehow appeared back in her life.

"Do you want him to come over again?"

Lauryn gave her a sleepy smile. "He said he'd help me build a sandcastle on the beach one day and take me out for crab legs."

"Sounds like a lot of fun."

More memories resurfaced, flipping between long days beside Italy's seaside and her senior year at Portland State. The only two men she'd ever loved.

Jason had been her college sweetheart and first love. Fun and full of life, he'd proposed to her one spring afternoon, and she'd said yes, eager to live the rest of her life beside him. But fear from watching her father walk out on her and her mother had slowly crept into their relationship and, like a weed-choked garden, had eventually become the unwanted motivator that had caused her to run. So instead of walking down the aisle that summer, she'd escaped to Europe and buried herself in art, culture and fourteenth-century Italy.

Having Jason walk back into her life might have thrown a kink into her normally structured routine, but despite his resurrecting long-lost memories, she wasn't ready to take a chance on love again. She'd done that with Quinton and had ended up trying to pick up the shattered pieces of her heart when he'd died. That loss was enough to convince her that allowing herself to fall in love again wasn't worth the risk.

Tonight had shaken those beliefs because Jason had reminded her how much she missed someone to help share the burdens of life, to encourage her and to help her deal with her frustrations. For months, she'd strived to rely on her faith to be that anchor, but while her trust in God had deepened, she still struggled to let her spiritual life fill the void in her heart that Quinton had left. Trust in God and a Savior might have become more real to her, but she still missed the companionship she'd found with Quinton.

Which oddly enough was the very reason why she couldn't let Jason back into her heart. Today had reminded her just how vulnerable she really was, but Jason wouldn't be here forever. He'd managed to appear for a moment, but when all of this was over, they'd both go back to living their own separate lives.

She let out a slow breath as she walked into the living room to double check that the doors were locked and the alarm set. The wooden wall clock ticked in the background. A dog barked outside. Lights of a passing car reflected through the window. All familiar and yet at the same time, nothing about these past two days held any degree of familiarity. Stories of murder and deceit were things she watched on the ten o'clock news or an episode of *CSI*. Not in real life.

Danielle pulled back the curtains covering the front window and stared into the darkness broken only by a lone streetlight. No matter what happened, she wasn't going to give into the fear threatening to engulf her. That would only let their hacker win…and leave her feeling even more vulnerable and violated.

At her computer desk she hesitated before clicking on the get mail button. Nothing. She'd checked her secondary account and work account earlier as well as the junk folder. Not only had the police launched their own investigation, Jason had assured her he would use every resource possible to track down the email's author. But being invisible online wasn't hard. Which meant finding their hacker could very well prove impossible.

Danielle set the mouse down. Jason had been right. There was nothing more she could do tonight. Staying up and worrying was only going to make things worse. She needed to take a long hot shower, read her Bible and spend some time in prayer. She started to shut down her computer, then stopped. Jason's leather wallet sat on the edge of her desk.

She pulled her cell phone out of her back pocket and scrolled through her contact list where he'd programmed his number into her phone. Pushing the call button, she waited for Jason to pick up, wishing she didn't feel so relieved for the excuse to call him.

Jason strode through the lobby door of the Pacific Cove Inn, hoping he'd made the right decision leaving Danielle alone. The rhythmic crashing of the waves faded as the automatic door shut behind him. Inside he barely noticed the busy geometric carpet competing with sea-green beach decor and black-and-white seashell photographs adorning the walls. Staying with his father was always an option, but he'd decided it would be better to sleep in town instead of the isolated cabin north of town. And after what had transpired today, he was thankful he'd made that decision. No matter what baggage they carried between them, if anything happened to Danielle he'd never forgive himself.

To the left of the lobby, the hotel restaurant smelled of hamburgers and greasy fries—a reminder of how much he'd enjoyed the meal of mac and cheese with Danielle and Lauryn. For a few minutes, they'd somehow managed to avoid talking about their own rocky past along with what had transpired today. But that hadn't lasted. The reality of what had taken place today still lay too close to the surface.

Which was why he'd hated to leave her. And hated even more that he didn't know what else he could do to make things okay. He'd gone over and over what he needed to say to Garrett when he found him, but had never anticipated not getting to talk to him again. Now he was contemplating a funeral, the urgent need to track down a con man and murderer, and finding a way to protect the woman he used to love.

His cell rang. He pulled the phone out of his pocket as he started toward the hotel elevators.

It was Danielle.

His brow narrowed as he answered the call. "Hey. Are you okay?"

"I'm fine. I just realized that you left your wallet here."

He felt his back pocket where he always kept his wallet and frowned. The distraction of everything that had happened—and even Danielle herself—had clearly affected him. Somehow, he was going to have to find a way to stay focused despite his emotional involvement in the situation. He turned down the hallway toward his room. At least she was okay.

"I won't need anything out of it tonight. Do you mind if I pick it up tomorrow?"

"Of course not."

He searched for something else to say, not ready to say goodbye. "You sound tired."

"I am, but I'll be okay. Emotionally everything seems to be hitting at once now that I'm here alone."

"I feel the same way. I think what happened is finally beginning to sink in…but I'm also worried about leaving you alone."

There was a pause on the line. She'd agreed to let him go to the bank in the morning with her, but he wasn't sure how much of his help she wanted. He wasn't a part of her life, and she was used to doing things by herself. Just because they shared a past didn't mean she wanted him coming to her rescue. And neither did he want his heart broken again. But he still couldn't shake the feeling that he was responsible for her. Or the fact that he wanted to be the one to make sure she was okay.

"I'll be fine," she added. "Really. I spoke to my neighbors like I promised. They're good friends and are home if I need anything. The house is locked, alarm set, Lauryn's tucked into bed and sound asleep…we'll be fine."

Fine seemed relative. All he felt like he'd accomplished tonight was dredging up more frustration and guilt. Garrett's parents had called while working on the funeral arrangements. It was something you never plan to do for your own child. And he still didn't have any answers for them.

The guilt returned as he skipped the elevator and took the stairs two at a time to the third floor. If he'd pressed Garrett more, and asked more questions, they might be dealing with a simple case of fraud, not murder. He shook away the self-recriminations. Whatever Garrett had been involved in, he'd made his own choices. More than likely, there was nothing Jason could have done to have changed any of it.

"Any more emails?" He started down the narrow hallway toward his room. She seemed to understand his need to stay on the line, even through the moments of silence when his thoughts were anything but silent.

"Nothing, though if I were our hacker, I would think that the lower the profile I keep the better considering the police are paying a lot more attention to a murder case. He's not going to want to take any chances of being tracked down at this point."

"You're probably right." Jason slid his key card into the slot on his door. "Murder isn't usually in the mark of a con man, which also means that he's veered from his normal, familiar territory."

Inside, the queen-size bed pillows had been fluffed and the turned-down bed reminded him that he was exhausted. All he wanted to do was escape into a dreamless sleep. He'd take a couple of over-the-counter sleeping pills to ensure he got to sleep, because tomorrow he needed to feel rested enough to deal with the mess Garrett had left behind.

Jason let the hotel room door shut behind him, dropped his keys onto the short counter beside the coffeepot then paused on the dark blue carpet.

Something wasn't right.

"Jason?"

"I'm here, it's just that…"

He studied the room, then turned toward the bathroom. The light was on, the closet door open. There was a sock on the floor he knew he hadn't left there.

The maid wouldn't have done any of those things.

"Jason, what is it?"

"Someone's been in my room." Or was still in his room. "Just a second."

He searched the bathroom, under the bed and outside on the balcony. Nothing. Whoever had been here was gone.

"Did they take anything?"

He rifled through his suitcase that had been opened inside the closet and left in a shambles. The dresser drawers were partially ajar, though he hadn't even taken the time to unpack when he arrived yesterday. He hadn't figured he'd be here long enough to move in. "It doesn't look like it."

Anything of value he'd kept with him.

And he'd packed light, only expecting to be here for a couple of days. His plan had been to simply find Garrett, confront him then get him back home. Two... three days max. At the moment he had no idea when he'd be able to return home to his apartment. He wasn't leaving until he had answers. Or until he knew Danielle was safe.

The need to protect her intensified. He'd seen the look of fear in her eyes as he'd left tonight. She'd been through a lot over the past couple of years, but he also knew that the feelings simmering inside him toward her were nothing more than the result of two people being thrown into a tense situation. Emotionally, he might feel the need to keep his distance, but that didn't change the fact that he still cared what happened to her.

"They had to have been after Garrett's evidence," he said.

"You need to let the police know what has happened, because after tonight it's clear Garrett must have said something to him to make him believe that either you or I have it."

"You're right."

Jason opened the sliding glass door to his balcony and stared out at the moon and its silvery reflection across the dark waters. There was something calming and familiar about these picturesque surroundings where he'd spent holidays and summer vacations hiking along the coast, exploring craggy rock structures, sandboarding and going on adventurous jaunts.

Back then, they'd been convinced they'd live forever.

"Do you remember the summer we went for a ride on that dune buggy?" There was a slight pause on the line as he waited for her answer.

"How could I forget? I thought I was going to die that afternoon."

"We were lucky that day."

The dune buggy accident had happened in slow motion. They'd hit the side of a sand dune, flipping the buggy. He thought he'd lost her in that careless act, but they'd managed to walk away with only a few bruises.

"I felt powerless when that buggy crashed…and that's how I feel right now." He sat down on the edge of the bed. "Like everything's out of control. I don't know where Garrett hid the evidence, don't know what this guy wants— or for that matter how much damage he's already done. We've got to figure things out and the clock is ticking."

FIVE

Danielle stood inside the display window of The Bamboo Closet the next morning, adjusting a shimmering gold fabric panel while Sarah eyed the display from the front. Deciding on what color backdrop matched best with the new shipment of plump, embroidered cushions was the last thing she'd planned to be doing this morning.

That and having to go to the bank to track down over a quarter of a million dollars of stolen money.

She grabbed the thin metal chain of an amber Moroccan lantern lying on the floor beside her and headed up the short ladder.

Money wasn't the only thing that had kept her tossing and turning throughout the night. There was also Jason. She hadn't been prepared for the added complication of yearning for the one man—besides Quinton—who'd ever captured her heart.

Somehow, though, his broad shoulders, five-o'clock shadow and that familiar half smile that always managed to coil her heart into a tangled pile of emotions had managed to drift in and out of her dreams all night long.

Jason had been right about one thing. Like that terrifying moment when their dune buggy had flipped, and she'd realized there was nothing either of them could do to stop it, her world had managed to spin out of control. And she had to find a way to set things right again.

"Danielle?"

She glanced down at Sarah from atop the ladder and finished hanging the lantern, wondering how long she'd been trying to get her attention. "Sorry."

"You okay?"

"I've just got a lot on my mind." Danielle stepped back off the ladder to study her work. "How does it look so far?"

"I love it." Sarah gave a nod of approval. "Especially the added touch of the throw pillows and lanterns. The bright oranges and yellows are very Moroccan and definitely eye-catching."

"Let's hope so, because window dressing was Rae's thing." Danielle dragged the teak armchair an inch closer to the long panel, thankful Sarah hadn't decided to quit, as well.

"How about another lantern in that bare spot," Sarah suggested. "A blue one this time."

Danielle scooted the ladder two feet toward the window, then grabbed another lantern. "I still don't understand what happened to Rae. She's always been so dependable."

Until she quit—without any warning—in the middle of dressing the shop's front window.

"Did you try calling her again?" Sarah tugged on a lock of her bleached-blond hair.

"Three times, but either her phone is off, or she's not answering. All I know is the message I got on my answering machine. Her boyfriend broke up with her, and she's moving back to Texas."

"All in the course of twenty-four hours." Sarah shook

her head. "If you ask me, their breakup was inevitable. I never did like that guy…."

"He was a bit…rough." Danielle readjusted the bottom edge of the fabric. "But I thought she liked living here."

"So did I."

"Maybe I shouldn't be surprised. Rae always was a bit impulsive, and love tends to do crazy things with your emotions." Danielle gnawed at her lower lip, trying to ignore the similarities to her own life. "We'll have to look at hiring someone else."

"Let me know what I can do to help."

"Thanks, I will." Danielle stepped down from the low platform to grab one of the terra-cotta pots from the pile of accessories she'd laid on the floor and set the piece on the top of the matching teak coffee table. Her finances were in ruins, and here she was arranging furniture and the latest home accent decor.

Sometimes life made no sense.

Danielle glanced at her watch. "Listen, it's almost a quarter to nine. I've got to be at the bank when it opens. Kate called and said she'd be a few minutes late, but if the two of you don't mind keeping things going today, it would help me."

"Anything wrong?"

"Yes, actually." Danielle stood up and tried to stretch the kinks out of her back. "It looks as if someone just stole a huge chunk of money from me."

"What?" Sarah almost dropped the mosaic vase she was holding. She set it down on the wooden table then looked back at Danielle. "How in the world did that happen?"

"They found a way to transfer over a quarter of a million dollars from my home equity account."

"Wow. I can't believe someone would do that. What are you going to do?"

"A friend of mine is meeting me at the bank. Hopefully, with his help, we can sort all this out."

Sarah placed a narrow glass bowl with colored stones next to the vase then stepped back to look at her work. "Who is this guy?"

"He's an old friend from college."

"Just a friend?"

Danielle swallowed her irritation as she started folding up her stepladder. "Yes, just a friend."

"Sounds interesting." Sarah sat down on the edge of the platform and picked up the can of cola she'd left on the floor. "When's the last time you actually went on a date?"

"On a date?" Danielle shook her head. "We're not going out, if that is what you are implying. He owns a company that works in online security and has offered to help me fix this mess I'm in. Period."

"So you're telling me that the flush on your cheeks has nothing to do with this guy?"

"No." Danielle gave the hanging fabric one last tug. Just because the blue-eyed, six-foot-two bachelor had swept in like Prince Charming to save the day didn't mean she had to swoon like some fairy-tale princess. Because there was one big problem with this scenario: there was much more at stake than merely giving her heart away again.

Fifteen minutes later, Danielle was crossing the parking lot in her gray dress pants and purple cardigan, praying she felt as confident as she looked—and that the bank transfer they'd discovered last night would be easily rectified. Hadn't she already survived one of life's curveballs that had left her a widow before she turned thirty?

Which was why she needed to believe that life was going to continue as usual with routine things like taking care of Lauryn and the shop, dinner with friends from church and hanging out with her mom. At least that was what she wanted to believe. Staying up until 1:00 a.m. scouring the internet for everything she could find on recent cases of bank fraud and identity theft had left her head numb with the reality that more than likely there weren't going to be any easy solutions.

As promised, Jason was waiting outside the main door of the bank, holding two cups of coffee. She eyed his profile where he stood at the top of the stairs, wearing jeans paired with a button-down shirt and jacket. How could this ruggedly handsome man make her heart skip a beat like she was twenty again? Except he wasn't here just for her. He wanted to find out the truth behind his friend's murder, as much as she did.

He handed her one of the coffees. "It's not an espresso and this isn't Venice, but I was told that the local gas station has the best brew in town. And it's fresh."

"Thanks." She took the hot drink and felt her cheeks warm. He'd always known how to make her smile. "I think I heard the same rumor."

"So, are you ready for this?"

"Ready to find out how the bank lost over a quarter of a million dollars?" She took a sip of her coffee and frowned. Having a bank manager confirm the transfer was only going to make the situation all the more real. "I just want to get this over with."

He brushed against her arm as they started for the front door together, forcing her to try and ignore the tingling sensation it evoked. As much as she wanted to fight it, Jason still made her heart pound and her breath catch.

"Everything okay at the store?"

Danielle caught the concern in his voice as she looked back up at him. "I had an employee quit this morning. I can't help but question the timing."

He crinkled his forehead. "That is a bit odd. I've got Philip tracking down who might have hacked into your accounts. I can have him do a background check on the employee if you'd like, but to be honest, I don't think it's going to be easy finding this guy."

"Why?"

He swallowed the last sip of his coffee, then dumped the empty cup into the trash bin near the bank entrance. "We're not dealing with your typical scam artist. We're dealing with a professional. He—or she—knows enough about you to take on your identity far beyond the normal trail of paperwork. And he knows how to cover his tracks."

Danielle pressed her lips together. "So what now?"

"We talk to the bank and find out exactly what we are up against."

They slipped inside the glass doors of the bank behind a woman dressed in a pink jogging outfit. Danielle took in the sleek feel of the bank's interior with its modern furniture, sharp angles and polished floor. She couldn't remember the last time she'd actually stepped inside. Internet banking and late drive-through hours made avoiding the teller lines inside far too easy.

A minute later, they located the manager, Mrs. Wang, along a row of uniform desks, all with gold nameplates. The woman sitting behind the desk looked ultraprofessional in her tan pant suit and white starched shirt that peeked over the jacket's collar, making Danielle realize just how thankful she was for Jason's presence.

Mrs. Wang looked up from her computer and offered

a bright smile as if to emphasize that everything was fine in the world. "Can I help you?"

"My name's Danielle Corbett, and this is Jason Ryan." She forced a weak smile in return. "I have questions regarding a $350,000 transfer from my home equity account that I never authorized."

"That is a serious accusation." The woman's smile faded slightly. "Please. Both of you take a seat."

Danielle slid into the plump leather chair she was offered beside Jason and set her coffee on the edge of the woman's desk. "It wasn't meant to be an accusation. Simply a fact."

Mrs. Wang tapped her pen against the desk. "I'll need to see some identification first, please."

Danielle pulled her Oregon driver's license from her wallet and slid the card across the table, wondering if the photo ID would be enough to convince the woman that she really was Danielle Corbett, and that she hadn't authorized the bank's transaction.

Mrs. Wang studied the photo then punched a few numbers into the computer. The printer on the edge of the desk began to hum, and a moment later, she handed Danielle the printout. "You can check over the statement, but the details of the transaction are all here."

Danielle started at the top, looking for any indication that something was amiss with the bank's paperwork. Name, social security number, driver's license, home address…Danielle's stomach muscles cinched, competing with the wave of nausea that overtook her. Everything matched. Which meant the money had been transferred from her line of credit to some other account—probably offshore—where she'd never see it.

"Everything here looks to be in order, but…" Her voice rose in pitch as she handed the printout to Jason for him to double-check. "I assure you that I did not authorize this transaction."

"As you can see, Mrs. Corbett, the paperwork is quite straightforward."

"Mrs. Wang, we can see what the computer says, but the bottom line is that this transaction was never authorized." Jason reached over and squeezed her hand, helping to counteract the deepening surges of frustration. "Can you tell me how this alleged transfer was made?"

"Yes, I remember this particular transaction actually." Mrs. Wang tapped her pen against her desk and narrowed her brow. "Mrs. Corbett came in to arrange the withdrawal. We later called her house to get the confirmation because the approval amount changed after I received it."

"But I never spoke to anyone here." Danielle closed her eyes momentarily, drawing strength from Jason's calming presence and the anchor of his touch. How had he become the only thing in her life that made sense? "You don't believe I'm really Danielle Corbett, do you?"

Mrs. Wang slid her pencil behind her ear. "To be honest, I don't know what to think."

"Why would I come in when the money was already transferred? That doesn't even make sense. If I already had the money, as you say I do, there would be no reason for me to be sitting here." Danielle tried to take in a calming breath, but nothing about the situation made sense. "Who spoke to woman who made this request?"

Mrs. Wang glanced at an empty desk across the room. "Sam Shepherd. He's out today."

Of course. Danielle let go of Jason's hand and grabbed her beaded gray handbag off the floor and pulled out her second round of ammunition. Identification papers. She dumped the file folder she'd pulled from her locked safe at home. Birth certificate, marriage license, social security card, passport....

Mrs. Wang sifted through the pile, still looking flustered. After a few moments, she made photocopies then pushed the papers back across the desk to Danielle. "I will add these documents to your file. If you believe this is a case of identity theft, you will need to file an incident report with the police. Secondly, you will need to send us a certified letter laying out exactly what has happened. We will then do our own investigation into the matter."

"How long with that take?" Jason asked.

"Typically, ten days to discover if there is a problem. In the meantime, I can flag your account and contact you regarding any unusual activity."

Which meant there was nothing left to do for the moment.

Danielle slung her bag over her shoulder and stood to leave. Something caught her eye, stopping her midstep. She turned back to Mrs. Wang. "What about the surveillance cameras? Whoever came in to authorize the transaction wasn't me, and your cameras should be able to prove it."

Mrs. Wang's gaze avoided Danielle. "The bank's policy is to cooperate with law enforcement who have a court order."

"Then we will ensure that they get one."

Danielle headed out of the bank at Jason's words without looking back, wondering why she was the one who felt like the guilty party.

SIX

"Danielle, wait." Jason caught up with her halfway down the bank steps.

"This is crazy." She dumped the rest of her coffee into the trash then turned to face him. "How did I suddenly become the bad guy here? I feel like I'm being scrutinized for something I didn't do. Isn't it the bank's business to ensure that my money is safe, and that someone can't just swoop in and wipe out my account? You saw that woman's face. She didn't believe me."

"It doesn't matter what she believes at this point. There are certain protocols she has to follow no matter what her personal thoughts are. The bank will investigate your claims and, if everything goes the way it should go, you'll be able to put this behind you."

"After a bank investigation and a pile of police reports?" She started across the parking lot. "What if they don't rule in my favor? What if they don't believe I didn't have something to do with this?"

He stepped in front of her halfway down the row of cars, turned her gently toward him, then rested his hands against her shoulders. "I know this isn't easy, but let's not borrow trouble."

"I'm trying not to." Her shoulders relaxed slightly as

she looked up at him, her breathing still ragged. "But what do we do next? I can't just wait ten days for the bank to sort things out."

He shot her a half smile and brushed away a strand of her hair. What he really wanted to do next was kiss her.

"I thought we could go out for breakfast," he said instead.

"Breakfast? We're in the middle of a crisis and all you can think about is food." She shook her head. "If I didn't know better I'd say you're not taking this seriously enough."

"Just answer one question for me." He folded his arms across his chest. "What did you eat today?"

"I made some oatmeal for Lauryn—"

"I asked what did you eat today?"

She frowned. "A cup of freshly brewed coffee and half a cup of a gas station variety."

He quirked a brow. "That's what I thought."

"Jason, I don't have time—"

"I take this entire situation very seriously, but with all that is happening, you have to take time to take care of yourself."

Ten minutes later, Jason picked up the plastic menu sitting in front of him and tapped it against the wooden table. Danielle's choice of restaurants wasn't bad, though he preferred his regular spot that offered the simple choice of one flavor of coffee—black with cream and sugar on the side. Not that it really mattered, he supposed.

Danielle slid into the bench across from him. She shoved a strand of her silky, cinnamon-brown hair behind her ear and shot him a sheepish grin. "As I remember, you always did think that eating was the solution to everything."

"But I'm right this time, aren't I?"

She grabbed one of the menus. "I suppose I am hungry."

"Good. Because what the hotel constitutes as breakfast, and what I constitute as breakfast turned out to be two completely different things. Which means I'm hungry, too."

"Sounds as if your new elitist taste buds are another thing that has changed."

He smiled, enjoying the friendly banter between them. "Like you, I run a business which means I have a certain...reputation to keep up."

"Late night dinners overlooking the Columbia River for your upscale clients, catered meals for your executives in the boardroom."

He had to laugh at her snooty impression. "Exactly."

"So you enjoy running a business?"

"I love it, actually. I have the freedom to expand in whatever way the market decides to go, and I certainly don't miss the bureaucracy and politics I'd be dealing with in a bigger company."

"I can't help but feel as if I'm dragging you away from your work." She started into the apology he didn't need or want from her.

"I've yet to turn down a damsel in distress." *Especially the one woman who'd always been irresistible to him.*

Another look at the menu helped rein in his meandering thoughts. Pancakes, waffles, omelets.... "I meant it when I said that we are in this together."

"Okay...then I won't feel bad."

"What do you want to eat?" he asked, gazing across the table at her.

She scanned the menu. "Something light. I'm not sure how much my stomach can handle."

The waitress stopped at their table, interrupting any

further discussion for the moment. The tall, thin brunette filled up Jason's coffee then stood ready to take their order.

Danielle handed the menus to the waitress. "I'll have the fruit salad."

"That will get you through the next what…hour? You've got to eat something substantial." He caught the stubborn rise of her chin and turned back to the waitress. "Give us two orders of waffles with hash browns, and an extra side of bacon and sausage with each."

"Jason…" Danielle stared at him as the waitress walked away. "Are you seriously ordering for me again? And what's with the extra bacon and sausage?"

He leaned forward and smiled at her. "If I remember correctly that used to be your Saturday morning staple back in college." He held up his hands. "But even if your taste in breakfast has changed, what hasn't changed is the fact that you need to eat."

Her expression softened slightly. "You're impossible, you know, and besides that how do you know that I still like bacon?"

"Because everyone loves bacon, and college wasn't that long ago."

"Long enough that an extra side of bacon and sausage doesn't simply disappear after an hour at the gym. Today—"

"Trust me. You don't have anything to worry about today, either."

She ducked her head, but he didn't miss the red blush that spread across her cheeks.

While her expression hinted at the fact that part of her world might have just caved in, he didn't miss the fact that she still looked just as beautiful as the day they first met. But as much as he didn't want to notice the dark color of her eyes, the soft curls of hair against her neck or her tanned skin against her purple shirt there was one thing he couldn't afford to forget. Whatever past they'd once shared together had to stay in the past because ten years was a long time. And like it or not, he was no longer a part of her life.

For the moment, though, they had more pressing things to consider. They were going to need to go through Garrett's accounts, evaluate security risks to determine if the company had been compromised and find a way to get their hacker to stop preying on Danielle.

Danielle eyed the ridiculous amount of food the waitress had just set in front of them while fighting the queasiness that had settled in her stomach. She took a sip of her coffee, wishing she could wash down the fear along with her breakfast. She could pretend this was all simply going to disappear, but she'd seen the truth reflected in Jason's eyes. This was more than a routine case of identity theft. She'd just been scammed out of over a quarter of a million dollars—and that wasn't the only thing that frightened her. Someone knew enough about her habits, personality and private information to have been able to walk into her bank and convince the manager that they were her.

Jason prayed over the food, then winked at her before digging into his plate of food. "I'm not planning to eat your breakfast, too, so you'd better get started."

She waved her fork in the air. "Were you always this bossy?"

"Even more so, probably."

Danielle shook her head. He'd always known how to lighten a stressful situation, but for the moment she needed more than a good laugh. She needed answers. "I want to know how something like this could happen."

"Will you eat?"

"I'll eat—at least some of it—I promise." She held up a bite of hash browns to make her point. Her stomach growled. Maybe she was hungry, after all.

"I'm not a computer guru like Garrett was, but I know enough to see that our hacker is very good at what he does. Few people realize how simple identity theft really is. A few numbers, a date of birth, a pile of recycled credit card applications... It's amazing what a pro can do with them."

The thought made her shudder. "So I make one mistake, or throw away something I shouldn't have, and bingo, I'm suddenly the target of a scam?"

"That kind of information isn't hard to find. All this guy needs is a trash can, a stolen wallet or perhaps a bribed employee, and he can become whoever he wants, whenever he wants. Lines of credit, brand-new vehicles, rented apartments—you name it."

Danielle poured boysenberry syrup across her buttered waffle and frowned. What she'd read online had left her leery, but vehicles and apartments? "You're kidding, right?"

"I wish I were. And unfortunately, by the time most victims discover the loss, there's nothing but a cold trail behind the perpetrator. On the positive side, thanks partly to Garrett's phone call, you found out before the bank started expecting payments."

Danielle tried to digest the facts as he threw them at her, but it was getting increasingly difficult. And one twist in particular stood out, possibly superseding even the financial loss—murder. She shoved the thought away.

"What about the phone call to my house? That wasn't me who answered."

Jason picked up his pen and drew a few lines on his napkin. "Most houses have a little gray box located on the outside of their house called a Network Interface Device."

"A Network Interface Device?" She shot him a blank look. "I might be able to decipher your…doodling, but you've just proficiently jumped beyond my knowledge of technology."

He frowned, but his eyes still sparkled. "Insulting my artwork now, are you?"

"Of course not. I remember how seriously you take your…art."

She used to have a collection of all the doodles he'd made into cards for her. Birthdays…Valentine's Day… their one-year anniversary…. She dropped her gaze at the memories. Clearly, the past was a place they both needed to avoid at the moment.

Jason cleared his throat, evidently feeling the same way. "Simply put, an NID is what connects your home telephone lines to the telephone company's network."

That she could understand. Even if she didn't like the sound of it.

"With a bit of computer background," Jason continued, "diverting a call to another phone is possible."

Danielle mulled over the implication. "Making that little gray box on the side of the house worth over a quarter of a million dollars."

He tapped his pen against the pad. "If Garrett hadn't called you, you wouldn't even know what had happened yet."

"So by the time I find out, the cash—and the perpe-trator—is long gone."

"With your money." Jason shoved his napkin aside as

the waitress refilled their drinks. "Do you have an alarm system?"

"At both my house and the store."

"Good."

Danielle wasn't sure she liked where the conversation was going. "Good because whoever did this is still watching me?"

"It's possible, depending on how much he thinks he can get out of you. There's also the chance that the guy's sitting in some tropical cabana a thousand miles from here."

That should make her feel better, but it didn't. Not when she knew her adversary was spending her hard-earned money.

She stared at her plate, knowing she needed to keep her emotions out of the equation. But the very idea that someone could have managed to steal this kind of money without her knowing it was enough to scare anyone. And unfortunately, she knew from experience that the old cliché that *life would never be the same again* could happen in an instant.

She finished half of her waffle and moved on to the hash browns, hungrier than she'd expected. He'd been right about her eating something. She wasn't going to be able to handle things—or be there for Lauryn—if she didn't take care of herself.

She sprinkled pepper onto the potatoes. "I've done enough research in the past twenty-four hours to know that identity theft can ruin a person financially."

"It can," he conceded, "but not always."

"Then tell me this? Who's going to end up repaying $350,000 to the bank? I have a feeling my nemesis isn't planning to pay up, and while my business might be going well, I don't have the extra monthly income the bank is going to demand on that kind of loan."

"I'll be upfront with you. There are thousands of victims like yourself who have been left to clean up the mess. It's completely unfair and wrong, but in the end someone has to pay."

"So what can we do to avoid that happening? If we can find the person who did it, the bank will have to believe me."

"It's not as easy as it seems." Jason started doodling on the side of his napkin. "The people involved in scams like this one are professionals. They know how to get in and out before the victim has a clue as to what's going on. It could be someone you know, but more than likely, it's a complete stranger."

A shiver trailed down Danielle's spine despite the warm room. She hated feeling vulnerable. Hated knowing someone had slipped into her sphere without her knowing it. "What about background checks on my employees?"

"Definitely. How many do you have beside the one who quite this morning?"

"Two others who work full-time, Kate and Sarah. Then I have several other part-time workers who come in during high season and holidays."

Jason added a spoonful of sugar to his coffee. The man obviously hadn't kicked the caffeine addiction she remembered. Or his habit of constantly doodling. "I'll also need a list of anyone you have regular dealings with."

"Of course." She dropped her fork onto her plate. The last time she remembered feeling this defenseless was when they'd told her Quinton was gone. Which was part of the reason she felt so conflicted over Jason's presence. No matter how real the stirred-up emotions he evoked in her, she was afraid to feel them again.

"Have you noticed anyone hanging around your neighborhood who shouldn't be there? Anyone following you or maybe spending a lot of time at your store?"

Danielle squeezed her eyes shut and searched her memory for anything out of place. She tended to study people for details, which meant she often ignored the bigger picture.

Danielle shook her head. "I haven't noticed anything out of the ordinary, though that doesn't mean I didn't miss it. My life is pretty hectic with Lauryn and the store."

"That's okay." His soothing voice spread through her like a balm. "We're going to find out who did this."

"I hope so."

"We'll find them. I might be a bit bossy—or determined as I prefer to call it—at times, but that habit can come in handy at times."

Danielle smiled. His determination was what she was going to need until this was over. "So what's our next move?"

"Well, we need to follow up on the police investigation and see if they've made any headway in the case. But I'd also like to look through your financial records. If there are any other discrepancies it might give us a place to start."

Danielle nodded. "I keep everything at my office at the store."

Jason snagged the bill from the table as the waitress set it down. "And if you'd like to go with me, I also need to visit Garrett's parents. I'm hoping they'll have a clue as to why their son was murdered."

SEVEN

While Jason spoke with Garrett's father in the garage, Danielle stepped into the middle of Garrett's sports-themed bedroom at his parents' house and took in the displays of silver trophies, ribbons and team banners. Seeing the home where he'd grown up helped to give insight into the man he'd once been, but for the moment her attention was drawn to the woman standing across from her. And the all-too-familiar look of loss in the older woman's eyes.

"Garrett was number twenty-four." Mrs. Peterson stood in front of one of her son's team photos hanging on the wall. "He was so tall and skinny back then, despite always eating like there was no tomorrow."

Danielle studied the team photo. Putting a name and history behind the body she'd pulled out of the ocean also made the situation all the more real.

"When he was in school, sports were his passion. Long-distance running and basketball in particular." Mrs. Peterson sat down on the blue-striped bedspread and ran her finger across his name engraved at the bottom of one of the trophies sitting on the nightstand. "He played basketball on the high school varsity team, then went on to play in college until he busted his knee. Shot any chances of going pro which he'd dreamed of his entire life."

"How did he handle that?"

"He had a rough time for a while. Besides running, basketball had become his life, and he'd never wanted to do anything else." She set the trophy back down on the nightstand beside her. "Eventually, he discovered he had a knack for computers and technology and went that direction. I think he enjoyed what he did. But now...I just keep asking myself what he could have gotten involved in that ended up costing him his life."

"I am sorry for your loss, Mrs. Peterson." Danielle struggled for the right words, knowing from her recent experience that there was no pat response. "I know all too well how difficult it can be to lose someone you love deeply. My husband was killed in an accident two years ago. It's taken me a long time to get past that initial grief and move on."

"I'm sorry to hear that. But you really do understand, don't you?" Mrs. Peterson stared at the photo. "Garrett always teased me that nothing has changed in this room since high school graduation. I loved being a mother, loved all the carpooling, track meets and scout meetings. Now I don't have a choice but to let him go."

Mrs. Peterson had just started down that road. Days of unquenchable grief that would eventually give way to a desire to embrace life again. But it was going to take time to get there.

"I'd planned to convert this into a guest room and nursery one day for my grandchildren," she continued. "My daughter has her own family, but Garrett never found anyone to settle down with."

Danielle caught the heartache in the older woman's

voice. "It's not always easy finding that one and only, is it?"

"He wanted a family, and I think the older he got the harder it became for him. He had high expectations and never seemed to meet women that fulfilled all of them." A tear rolled down her cheek. "Now we're planning a funeral and it's too late for any of that...."

Danielle reached over to pat the older woman's arm. "When was the last time you heard from him?"

"Over two weeks ago." Mrs. Peterson put the photo back and turned to Danielle. "He called to make sure we were still on to celebrate my birthday. He was a good son. Knowing how busy he was, I told him he didn't have to make the trip up here, but he insisted he wanted to."

Danielle shook her head. How had this ideal son gotten involved in a scam that had cost him his life? "Had Garrett been different lately?"

"He seemed... I guess *distracted* is the word I'd use for him over the past few months. He didn't come over as much as he normally did, but I knew he was busy with work and didn't think much about it."

"Did you know many of his friends?"

"Jason knew more who he hung out with than I do. He dated and did community service work which gave him a chance to meet people outside his work. You wouldn't know from just meeting him, but while he was a people person, Garrett was also intensely private. I've had people tell me that you could walk away from a conversation with him and realize how little you knew about him. Yet he'd take away your entire life story."

"I wish I could have met him."

A buzzer sounded from downstairs.

"That's the oven." Mrs. Peterson stood and wiped her

cheek with the back of her hand. "I put a cinnamon tea cake in before you got here."

Danielle followed her down the stairs to the kitchen, past the wall lined with childhood photos of Garrett and his sister through various stages of their lives—the kind of photos most kids wished their parents would hide away in a box in the attic.

The smell of cinnamon and sugar filled the kitchen as Mrs. Peterson pulled the cake from the oven. "My fridge is full of meals brought over from people at our church, but baking keeps me busy. And I need to stay busy."

"It smells wonderful." Still needing to find out something—anything—that might help them discover who was behind his death, Danielle steered the conversation back to Garrett while Mrs. Peterson set the cake on a rack and turned off the oven. "You mentioned he dated. Was he seeing anyone in particular lately?"

"It was a family joke, Garrett's dating habits." She leaned back against the tiled countertop. "I wanted grandchildren and told Garrett over and over that it would be nice to enjoy them before they put me into some old folks home. Of course, my daughter finally gave me a couple grandbabies, but commitment wasn't Garrett's strong suit…though I actually thought maybe he'd found someone. Someone serious, I mean."

"What happened?"

"Garrett came for dinner a few weeks back. There was something different about him. I teased him that there was a spring in his step. Like he was in love."

"Did he say anything to you?"

His mother nodded. "I asked him point-blank before he left to go home that night, and he admitted he'd met someone. That he even thought she might be the one he wanted to spend the rest of his life with. He seemed happy, yet at the same time very cautious, too." She smiled wistfully. "I remember mentioning to Bruce that I had this gut feeling Garrett had finally found *the one*. I just knew it. He'd gone out with dozens of girls, but this time was different. There was this glow in his eyes. A sense of contentment about him."

"But you never ended up meeting her?"

"No, and I never understood why." Mrs. Peterson began slicing the warm cake. "I asked him several times, but he always had an excuse. I got the impression she wasn't ready to meet his family, so I resigned myself to be patient."

"Do you know where he met her?"

"He told me he'd met her online, which worried me. I don't know anything about those online dating sites, but they certainly don't seem to be the place to meet someone decent. How do you really know who's behind the photo?"

Warning bells went off in Danielle's mind. "So he never met her in person?"

"I'm not really sure. All I know is when I asked him a couple weeks later when he was going to bring her home, he just brushed off the questions. He never spoke of her again, so I assumed something went wrong and it had turned into another one of his broken relationships. I guess now I'll never know."

Jason followed Bruce Peterson into the house from the garage. The older man had hoped to finish the Suzuki bike he'd been restoring with his son by Christmas, but without Garrett's help, Mr. Peterson had confessed he'd lost his motivation. Which was easy for Jason to understand. Being here in the familiar home where Garrett had grown up—without his friend here—only worsened the stinging reality that his friend was dead.

Inside the house, Mrs. Peterson had set plates of cake on the kitchen bar and was busying herself by pouring mugs of coffee…like she'd done dozens of times for him and Garrett before. He couldn't begin to count the number of summer barbecue's, Sunday dinners and Thanksgiving meals he'd spent here.

Jason lowered himself beside Danielle onto one of the bar stools and wondered how he should broach the next subject. But voicing his sympathy for one of his best friends wasn't the only reason he was here.

"I know this is very personal," he began. "But I need to know about Garrett's finances. Have you been able to find out anything?"

"We have started going through his accounts." Mr. Peterson glanced at his wife before continuing. "Garrett was always extremely meticulous with his record keeping, so that has made things easier. The first thing we noticed was a number of cash withdrawals over a period of about ten weeks, starting in June, that were taken from his savings account."

"How much money?" Danielle asked.

"Roughly $15,000."

Jason let out a low whistle. "That's no small lump of change."

"No, it's not." Mrs. Peterson stood across from him and jabbed at a piece of cake with her fork, before pushing the plate away. "And what makes it even more significant is that Garrett wasn't a big spender. He was frugal, always living on far less than he earned."

Jason nudged Danielle with his elbow. "We used to tease Garrett because of his brown bagging, frugal living habits. He definitely knew how to make just about anything last forever…but he'd also give the shirt off his back if needed."

"Which is why I don't understand why anyone would want to hurt him."

Mr. Peterson took his wife's hand and squeezed it. "You mentioned earlier that Garrett spoke to Danielle on the phone shortly before he died about being taken in by a scam. I'm assuming these cash withdrawals have something to do with this?"

"I think it does. I'll need to get specifics on the withdrawals and any other financial information to Philip, one of my IT specialists. He'll see if we can tie any of this together. What about Garrett's retirement fund, IRAs or other saving accounts?"

"Far as I can see, none of his other accounts were touched."

Danielle ran her finger around her coffee mug, her cake still untouched. "There is something else that stands out to me here, and that is the time frame. Assuming the information we have is correct, then at least two months have passed since Garrett's last withdrawal and yet something clearly happened this week to set off our killer."

Jason frowned. "Which implies that he was either dipping out of a different source of cash, or stopped the withdrawals."

"What about a stolen ATM card?" Mrs. Peterson threw out.

"He would have noticed that," Jason said. "This has gone on for at least what…four, maybe five months. If his card had been stolen, he would have reported and put a stop to them. I don't think this money was stolen."

Danielle set down her mug. "What if we're looking at this all wrong? What if it wasn't some random scam Garrett fell for, but instead a woman?"

Jason shook his head. "A woman?"

"Think about it. Mrs. Peterson told me that Garrett was

dating a woman, and while things didn't work out, for a time he was even considering marriage."

"Garrett was thinking about getting married?" Jason shook his head. How was it possible to work side by side with someone, day in and day out and not know something as important as that? "He would have told me."

"Maybe, but Garrett was private," Danielle continued. "Clearly private enough to keep a relationship from his close friends and family."

Jason still wasn't convinced. "Where did he meet her?"

"Online. So maybe instead of someone stealing his identity, they preyed on his emotions."

Jason took a sip of his now lukewarm coffee and tried to make sense of Danielle's theory. "Out of any scenario I can think of, I suppose that one makes the most sense, but I still say that Garrett was too smart to fall for something like that."

"The bottom line is that he fell for something…or someone," Danielle countered. "Granted I didn't know Garrett, but it seems like there is no dispute that at least $15,000 of his savings is gone, so unless he gambled the money away…"

"My son wasn't perfect, but I can't see him doing that, either," Mr. Peterson interjected with a deep frown.

Danielle looked to Jason. "Which means we need to find this woman."

If there really was a woman. But he wasn't willing to overlook any possibilities. "It's worth a try."

It still didn't answer why the cash withdrawals stopped. Or how Garrett had found out that Danielle was going to be next.

"What can we do?"

"You both know Philip. He's already working on the case, and if anyone can track down this guy—or woman as it might be—Philip can. I'll have him see if Garrett had been a part of a dating site."

"Wouldn't there be evidence on his computer?" Mr. Peterson asked.

"There should be, but if you want to hide a relationship, it isn't hard. Garrett could have easily had email addresses we don't know about and have been careful to cover his tracks."

Jason dug into a bite of cake. If Garrett had found out that he was being scammed by his online girlfriend, he'd be too embarrassed for anyone to know he'd been a victim. Which would explain why he'd never mentioned anything to Jason about his latest love interest. He knew how the cons worked. The victim was worked over slowly for weeks or months. Then the perpetrator continuously needs money for urgent medical bills, passports or phone bills in order to continue communicating with the victim.

But why stop the demands for money? And even more importantly, why kill Garrett?

Jason set his fork beside the plate. Because Garrett had known something. Something worth killing for. The same information the hacker was demanding.

"Jason?" Danielle's voice brought him back to the present. He'd share his ideas with Danielle later, after he had time to finish processing them.

"Sorry. We probably need to go, but I do have one last question." He turned back to Garrett's parents "Did he leave you any kind of package?"

"A package?" Mr. Peterson looked to his wife then shook his head. "No. Nothing. Why?"

"When I spoke to Garrett, he implied that he had sent me information. The problem is that I have no idea what it is, or where it could be."

Mrs. Peterson grasped Jason's hand. "Just promise us you'll find out the truth about what happened to our son. It's hard enough to lose a child, but this way…this isn't the way it's supposed to happen."

"You know I'll do everything I can to find out the truth behind Garrett's death."

A few minutes later, Jason stepped into the chilly afternoon breeze with Danielle. A storm was moving in along the horizon, bringing with it ribbons of dark clouds reflective of the anger raging inside him. None of this should have happened. Not to the Petersons. Not to Garrett. Not to Danielle.

"You okay?" Danielle stopped at the edge of the sidewalk and brushed her fingers against his arm.

Her touch pulled him back to the present. "Just lost in thought for the moment. The more I think about it, the more I believe you might be right about the dating angle. Romance scams aren't anything new, and while there are a few holes in our theory, this one seems to fit the best."

Danielle's phone rang as he reached to open her passenger-side door. She pulled it out and glanced at the caller ID. "Unknown caller."

"Do you want me to answer for you?"

"No…it's okay." She leaned against the side of the car and took the call. Jason tried to gauge her responses. Definitely not a close friend, but at least her voice wasn't tinged with fear.

"Who was it?" he asked once she'd hung up.

"A car salesman." She looked up and shook her head. "He called to let me know that there is a problem with the car I'm purchasing. Something about…something about my line of credit."

The phone dinged again as a message popped up on the screen.

Danielle handed him the phone, and Jason felt a chill run down his spine as he read the text.

Time's up.

EIGHT

Danielle slid into the cracked leather chair in front of the salesman's untidy desk, wondering what she was doing in the stale-smelling office of a used car lot thirty miles from home. At first introductions, she'd realized that convincing the balding man in the out-of-date suit they'd never met wasn't going to be easy.

"Mr..." Danielle shot up a prayer for wisdom, while glancing at the nameplate on his desk. "Mr. Audley. There seems to be some sort of problem. I have never been here before. Never bought a car from you."

It was just like the bank. Trying to prove she'd never been somewhere. Never visited this office. Never drove off the lot with one of his cars.

"I am sorry, Mrs. Corbett, but as I tried to explain to you on the phone, the problem isn't with the car...but your credit."

"Mr. Audley." Danielle looked briefly to Jason, tempted to let him handle the situation, but knew this was something she needed to tackle. "You're not listening to me. I have never been here. I didn't buy a car from you. I don't want to buy a car from you."

He shot her a patronizing smile. "You're not the first person to come back with second thoughts over a purchase. Buying a car is a huge investment, but to be honest that's not my problem at this point. I have your signature."

He slid the paper across the desk for her to see.

Danielle shook her head. "That isn't my signature—"

"What that means simply is that your interest rate will be higher than we first quoted."

Danielle shoved the paper back across the table. She was tired of going in circles. "Mr. Audley, I need you to stop and listen to me. I didn't sign this paper, and I don't have your car. I'm not sure who came in here pretending to me, but you were conned."

"Conned?" The man's brow narrowed as he started looking around the office. "What is this? One of those TV reality shows?"

"Hardly." Jason leaned forward and rested his hands against the edge of the desk. "But you can call it whatever you want. Swindled, bamboozled, duped…. Danielle isn't the one who came in here to buy a car."

Mr. Audley didn't look convinced. "I don't understand. All the paperwork was in order. Everything."

"What about surveillance footage?" Jason asked.

"Surveillance footage?" He shook his head. "I sell a lot of cars, but with the economy the way it is, I've had to cut both my profit margin and expenses over the past couple years. Doesn't leave much room for extras."

"Then let's start with this question," Danielle began. "The woman who signed for this car. What did she look like?"

"Mrs. Corbett, I might not be making a good profit, but business is good. Everyone wants to buy a used car. I had two dozen people come in here yesterday alone." Mr. Audley ran his hand across the back of his neck. "Multiply that by seven days a week, well…I'm sorry if I don't remember every face."

Jason glared at the car salesman. "Try to remember. It's only been a couple days."

"Fine." He scratched the back of his neck and directed his answer to Danielle. "She was your build, I suppose, and your same hair color. Dressed nice, but a bit vintage and wearing this…black, slouchy beanie. It seemed a bit out of place. I mean it's not really that cold outside."

Danielle looked at Jason. "Trying to avoid the camera?"

Mr. Audley looked up again. "This really isn't some joke?"

"No." Jason and Danielle responded at the same time.

"Did she leave with the car?" Danielle continued.

"Yes."

"We'll need the make, color, plate number…anything you've got." Jason added.

"Of course."

Jason was right. They'd probably ditched the car, but any info they could pass on to the police was worth a try.

"Was there a man with her?"

"No. You…she came alone." His already pasty skin had paled. "What do you suggest I do now?"

"We'll be in touch, but you might want to file a report with the police." Jason stood up. "Because trust me when I say that we want to catch whoever is behind this as much as you do."

Danielle's stomach clenched as she followed Jason across the gravel parking lot toward his car. "I'm not sure what we accomplished in there."

"We proved there is a woman involved."

A drop of rain splattered against her nose then ran down her cheek. Jason wrapped his arm around her and hurried her to the car, managing to help loosen the tangled knot of nerves in the process.

Danielle's phone rang as Jason pulled out of the parking lot. She checked the ID. Unknown caller. Whoever it was, this wasn't going to be good news.

"So have you finally realized that I'm serious?" The caller's voice resonated deep and scratchy.

"Who is this?"

"You know who this is."

"You have the car?" she asked.

"I thought I should show you exactly what I could do." She mouthed *It's him* to Jason. "I don't understand."

"Really? Let me put it another way, then. Your twenty-four hours are up."

"We don't have what you want," she insisted. "I can't produce something I don't have."

"That's not what I was told, which means I will continue to assume that you are lying."

Danielle closed her eyes and drew in a shallow breath. Convincing him she wasn't lying appeared to be useless. At some point they had to gain the upper hand.

"That is why I want you to see how I can get to you. Anywhere. Anytime. Don't do anything that could make things worse for you. Just get me what I want. It's that simple."

"And if I still can't get what you want?"

"I suggest you do, because at this point, I know everything I need to ruin you. I'll give you another twenty-four hours, but after that, I won't play nice anymore."

Danielle shoved her phone into her pocket as a wave of nausea flooded her stomach. "I need to get out of the car."

"Danielle?" Jason pulled the car on to one of the lookouts above the ocean. "What did he say?"

"I can't do this anymore."

* * *

Jason hurried after her as Danielle jumped out of the car and started down a narrow embankment toward the sea. Even though he also felt like running, somehow he was going to have to convince her that running away wasn't an option. That the only way they were going to win this was by staying focused.

When he caught up to her, she was leaning over facing the sea, hands braced against her thighs while the wind whipped at her hair.

"Breathe slowly, Danielle." He moved in front of her and rested his hands against her shoulders, hoping the rain would hold off. "Tell me what just happened. What did he say?"

She shivered in the chilly afternoon breeze. "He knows where I am, Jason. He can email me, call me.… He bought a car under my name just to show me that he's in control, and I'm not."

"Let me see your phone."

She fumbled to pull it out of her pocket.

"I'll have Philip see what he can do to trace the call, but there is a good chance he was using a burn phone."

She shook her head. "A burn phone?"

"The kind they use all the time in the movies. For the most part they are untraceable, especially when used as disposable."

She stood up slowly and pulled her hair away from her face. "I'm sorry."

"Why? Because you feel vulnerable? Everything you're feeling right now is normal and none of this is your fault."

Even he was at a loss as to what to do. Philip could only work so fast on the technical side, and even when they did make progress, it felt as if they were always a step behind.

"At some point, he's going to make a mistake, and we will catch him."

Tears pooled in her eyes. "And until then?"

"We keep trying to figure things out." He ran his thumb down her cheek.

"What if we don't figure things out in time?"

As much as he wanted to, he couldn't promise her everything would turn out all right. He'd learned the hard way from their own rocky past that burying your head in the sand to avoid the truth didn't change anything. "All we can do is take things one step at a time."

"I just hate that I can't fix this." She looked up at him. "I hate that I can't put a stop to what he's doing. Hate thinking that at some point, I left a password laying around, or a bank statement, or trusted the wrong person."

"Whoa. Sometimes, no matter how careful we are, someone still manages to take advantage of us. That's part of the consequences of the fallen world we live in. But it doesn't make it your fault."

Danielle shivered. He needed to get her home where she could get warm, but he realized she also needed some time to work through the emotions she was experiencing. Just as he needed to get a handle on the feelings churning through him. Feelings he'd vowed to leave in the past.

He pulled off his jacket and draped it around her shoulders. "You're not alone, Danielle. You've got a strong support network at church, your mother, Lauryn. And I promise to do everything I can to help you through this."

He gathered her into his arms and felt her shallow breathing against his neck. She was shaking, as much from fear as from the cold. After a minute she began to relax against his shoulder. It would be so easy to fall for her again. If only the circumstances were different, and he didn't still carry with him the scars from her walking out on him all those years ago.

"I just don't know how to do this." She pulled back and wiped away tears from her cheek. "He knows everything about me. He can hack into my accounts, steal my money...whatever he wants. And if he can get to me, he can get to Lauryn. I'm scared, Jason. I don't think I've ever been so scared in my life."

She sat down on a long piece of driftwood and stared out across the ocean. There might not be anything he could say to fix things, but at least he could be here for her.

"What else do you feel?"

"Mad that that someone couldn't care less that what he is doing could ruin my life all for the sake of greed. Is making a fortune really worth ruining someone's life—or for that matter is what he wants worth someone losing their life? I just don't understand."

"No, it's not worth it."

"He made his point, Jason. He can get to me, and I don't even know who he is. How can I stop someone I can't see?"

She looked up at him, her expression more one of sadness than fear now. "When Quinton died, my mother once told me that difficult things take a long time, and impossible things a little longer. I didn't think I'd ever get over losing him. I'd suddenly become a single mom and sole owner of the business we'd started together. For me the future seemed impossible. And like today, I couldn't see the end of the tunnel. Just a dark maze with no map to get to the other side."

"Which is why we have to figure this out. You always were the practical one, good at finding solutions."

"When all of the pieces are there. When I don't feel

as if I'm running for my life to stop things from getting worse." Danielle picked up a fistful of sand, then let the granules drain through her fingers. "But I have no idea where to look. No idea what he thinks I have or even how to find the information he wants. And in twenty-four hours, if I don't give him what he wants…I don't know what to do. The only thing I do know is that I can't let him win."

"Then we go over things again and again until we figure out the missing pieces." Jason rested his elbows against his thighs, watching the power of the waves crash against the rocks sprinkled along the shoreline. God was still in control—bigger than this situation. Even when circumstances made it seem that God was far away. "Garrett said something to this creep to make him think you—or possibly I—have what our hacker wants."

"So we've clearly been linked together. Did Garrett know about our past?"

They were both grasping for answers without any real direction, but it was better than doing nothing. "He knew I'd been engaged once, and that things didn't work out. Beyond that, I don't think the subject ever came up."

And he'd moved on. For the most part. Somehow, even after all these years had passed, he still found it hard to trust women. Or maybe it was simply his fears of not wanting to have his heart broken again.

Danielle drew in a deep breath and nodded. Color had returned to her cheeks. Partly because of the wind, but also because she'd decided that their nemesis wasn't going to win. This was the girl he remembered. Determined. Resolute.

Their hacker had chosen the wrong person to scam.

"Okay." She drew her knees up against her chest, watching the movement of the ocean and the dark clouds drifting silently across the horizon. "If what we are assuming is correct, there are at least two people working together."

"The woman Garrett told his mother about—the one who showed up at the car dealership and bank—and the man who called you."

Danielle nodded, her gaze intent and focused. "They're smart, computer-savvy and highly manipulative. They know how to stay under the radar and even vanish, since we can guess that it took Garrett a while to find them."

"They use different methods, identity theft and romance scams," Jason continued. "Nothing has shown up so far on Garrett's laptop, in his apartment or in his phone records so far."

"Which might mean that any communication he had with her was done on a separate email account or computer."

Giving them one more thing to look for.

Jason noticed the fatigue in her eyes. Like him, she probably hadn't slept well since all of this started and they'd missed lunch. Despite all that had transpired between them in the past, he still wanted to take care of her. "I'll tell you what. Philip has agreed to drive in later this evening so we can brainstorm some more in person, but in the meantime, we're both tired and need nourishment. The problem will still be here in an hour or two, and we'll both feel better if we eat. I'll even offer to fix dinner for you and Lauryn."

"Wait a minute." For the first time all day, she smiled. "You're actually offering to fix dinner? Your taste buds might have changed, but I remember you lived on ramen noodles and Cap'n Crunch in college, and there was definitely no cooking involved in that."

"As you said earlier, people change. Man cannot live

on instant soup and cereal his entire life, so I learned to cook."

"You learned to cook?" Her laugh took him by surprise. "Somehow I find that hard to believe."

"Wait a minute." He nudged her with his shoulder. "I think I should feel insulted."

"Actually, I'm pretty impressed."

"Then I'm definitely going to have to prove you right. How does lasagna and garlic bread sound?"

"You're talking homemade, with lots of garlic and cheese?"

"What else would I be talking about?" he drawled.

Jason took her hands and helped her up, expecting her to pull back once she was on her feet again. Instead, she looked up at him, her eyes wide, tinged with resolution…and longing?

No. Exploring one's feelings in the middle of a crisis wasn't a good idea. Anything she thought she might be feeling for him right now was colored by everything that was happening around them. She felt vulnerable and lost, and he had swept in to save the day.

He let go of her hands, wishing he could simply erase the feelings of rejection that still lingered. He focused instead on the wind that had picked up and the dark clouds moving in fast. They were going to get caught in the rain if they stayed out here much longer.

It had rained the day she left him. He remembered that moment like it was yesterday. Two weeks before their wedding, she'd met him at their favorite Chinese restaurant for lunch. She was out of breath when she ducked in, her hair and clothes damp from the rain despite the umbrella she carried. He'd expected to talk about their honeymoon plans. Money had been tight, but with his father's help, he'd bought a honeymoon package to the Caribbean. Five nights with the woman he planned to spend the rest of his life with.

Instead, she'd told him that she was sorry, but she couldn't go through with the wedding. There had been no real explanation. Just a straightforward apology.

He hadn't even seen the breakup coming.

Looking back, there had been signs. She'd seemed distant, but he thought she was busy with wedding plans. In the end, he'd been left to shoulder comments made by people he'd once thought of as friends as to what he'd done wrong.

He'd always hoped for an opportunity to ask her why, but that chance had never come. Until now.

But even now wasn't the right time.

He took a step back, wondering how he'd let his thoughts stray so far from their current situation.

She caught his gaze, the remnants of a smile still lingering on her lips. "Thank you."

"For what?"

"For making me laugh again. And simply for being here for me today."

Jason swallowed hard. Part of him almost wished circumstances hadn't brought them together. They'd both changed, but not enough to have completely extinguished the spark that used to be there between them. That unexplainable, unquantifiable equation when a man and woman knew they were meant for each other. At least that is what he'd believed. He'd thought they had been the perfect couple. Maybe that was why he'd never found anyone who could take the place of his first love.

They started back toward the car as the first raindrops fell. It shouldn't feel so natural to be this close to the woman who'd broken his heart. He shouldn't want to be this close to her, but somehow her presence helped to take the sting off the situation they were facing. Going through it together had put them back on the same team.

He stopped by the car and opened up the door for her, ignoring the desire to kiss her along with his tremulous feelings of needing to keep his distance. Only God knew what the future held, but for today, for right now, he couldn't help but be happy to have her back in his life again.

When all of this was over and all the pieces put back together maybe he'd finally understand what had happened that day. Maybe they could even discover a way to create something new between them. Until then, though, he needed to focus on what had brought them together in the first place. A deadly hacker who would stoop to anything—including murder—to get what he wanted.

NINE

"This is fantastic." Danielle took another bite of the tangy lasagna, thoroughly impressed with Jason's culinary skills. It had been a long time since a man had managed to impress her. Not only were most of the single men she knew clueless about cooking, they were too busy—or uninterested—to give Lauryn much notice.

Jason was clearly different on both accounts.

Besides agreeing to fix dinner, he'd also insisted she take as much time alone as she needed for a soak in the tub. When she'd finally joined them, he was in the middle of helping Lauryn tear lettuce for the salad.

Seeing the two of them laughing together was a scene that both thrilled and terrified her at the same time. She'd managed to get to a point in her life where she wasn't scared of living anymore. In a way, Quinton's death had taught her that. She'd learned firsthand that a life could be taken at the blink of an eye and change everything. Which was one reason why she was determined that she had to move on. But that decision in itself didn't always mean that the process was easy, and with all that had happened over the past few days, life's uncertainties, if anything, seemed stronger.

She broke off a piece of garlic bread and dipped it into

the sauce, choosing for now to focus on the positive. She nudged Lauryn with her elbow. "I have to say the two of you outdid yourselves. This is fantastic."

"Thanks." Jason smiled, looking as pleased with himself as Lauryn did. "It's an old family recipe."

The statement made her laugh. Since when had Jason started collecting family recipes? "I'm sorry. I didn't remember your having a domestic bone in you."

He shot her a grin. "I could have said it was a standby I use to impress beautiful women and their daughters, but I thought my answer was safer."

She held up her fork. "So this is a common occurrence? Impressing women—and their daughters—.with your talents in the kitchen?"

"Not at all." He winked at Lauryn. "This is the first time, actually."

Danielle struggled to repress the relief over the fact that impressing women with his culinary skills wasn't a normal part of his bachelor regimen. "Then I have a second question. Where did you learn to relate so well with kids?"

"My sister has a seven-year-old and a five-year-old which means I admit to playing Candy Land and spending Friday nights on the Wii."

"Hmm… What do you think about that, Lauryn?"

"I think he should make dinner for us every night!"

Danielle laughed. "Well, I don't know about every night. He might get tired of cooking for us after a while." Danielle felt the heat of a blush crossing her cheeks. "Lauryn is referring to my cooking. I'm sure you remember my cooking abilities, or shall I say, lack of them."

He popped a crouton into his mouth. "I don't ever remember criticizing your cooking."

"Good answer, but I'm sure you thought about it." Danielle smiled, liking the fact that he hadn't brought up her infamous charred chicken, or the time she caught a kitchen towel on fire. She gave up on romantic dinners for two that didn't include takeout early on in their relationship. "Let's just say that while I have made progress in the kitchen—not as much as you apparently—there are a few things that haven't changed all that much. We get by on a lot of ready-made meals and my mother's occasional donation to the cause."

She watched him take another serving of lasagna and savored the moment. In some ways, tonight was an opportunity to get to know him for the first time. Something she was finding she liked. Too much. He leaned across the table to help Lauryn get another slice of bread, not seeming to mind the smear of sauce on her sleeve or her buttery fingers. Which made Danielle have to try even harder to not stare at the dimple on his left cheek and how blue his eyes were.

She might not be ready to venture into what had happened between them, but Jason wasn't the same man. And she couldn't help but notice the subtle differences. He seemed more focused, more determined, and if it were possible, even more handsome than he'd been back in college. He hadn't lost that mischievous sparkle in his eye when he smiled, but without that, he wouldn't be Jason. Somehow he'd managed to balance his crazy fun side with a dose of reality.

And he'd been right about something else, as well. Spending a couple of hours away from the events of the past few days had given her a much-needed break from reality. Something she'd desperately needed after today. It felt good to laugh and forget—even for just a little while—what they were up against.

Somehow Jason had become the knight in shining armor she definitely wasn't looking for.

Danielle cleared her throat and turned back to Lauryn. "If you're finished, why don't you get your pj's on and brush your teeth, then I'll read to you before bed."

Lauryn nodded, then jumped down from the table, carrying her empty dish to the sink before running off down the hallway toward her room.

"She's adorable. Takes after her mother, you know."

Danielle picked up the empty plates, avoiding his gaze…and the fact that it seemed so natural to have him here. She started rinsing the plates before putting them into the dishwasher, wishing suddenly that they weren't alone. And that she didn't feel the intimacy of the moment.

"Being a single mom isn't easy, but you were right in what you said earlier. My mom's always there for me, and we are a part of a small church with members that have gone out of their way to help. Their support has made things doable." Lauryn had helped fill the empty spaces in her heart after Quinton died. "Thankfully, she's easy-going most of the time. She loves spending time with her grandmother, and coming with me to work…."

She was rambling, but it had been a long time since a man had tied up her heartstrings.

"Danielle? You okay?"

"Yeah. I'm fine. I was just…" *Thinking of how I like the way you make me feel, and realizing how I want to both explore this possibility and run away at the same time.*

She looked up at him and met his eyes, wondering how she'd managed to find herself in this position.

Lauryn arrived back in the kitchen dressed in her favorite pink Dora the Explorer pajamas and the bunny ears Danielle had bought for her on eBay. She was carrying a worn copy of *The Lion, the Witch and the Wardrobe* that they were reading together.

Danielle drew her in for a bear hug, avoiding the fluffy ears to kiss her on her forehead. "Did you brush your teeth?"

Lauryn nodded, then set the book down on the counter beside of Jason. "Wanna read me a chapter tonight?"

"Hmm…I think I could handle that." Jason looked up at Danielle. "Do you mind?"

"Of course not. I'll finish up in here."

Danielle watched as Jason tucked the book under his arm, and walked hand in hand with Lauryn into the living room. Then he sat down on the recliner with her and started reading. The little girl laughed at something Jason said, and Danielle moved to the doorway of the living room to watch him read the story.

She'd lost count of how many times her mother had tried to push her into dating. The last time had been the offer of a blind date with the son of a friend of a friend. But the timing had never seemed right. It was too soon, too uncomfortable and, with Lauryn, too complicated.

Danielle turned away from the image. Seeing her daughter snuggled against Jason's arm reminded her of what Lauryn had lost when she lost Quinton. All things she longed to give her daughter. But while she would never remarry simply to give Lauryn a father, her daughter wasn't the only one whose heart felt a void.

She went back to cleaning up until Jason came back into the kitchen.

"Hey, I left Lauryn on the couch. She fell asleep before I finished the chapter."

"I'm not surprised." Danielle closed the dishwasher and caught his tender gaze. She turned toward the living room, unable to ignore her heart's reaction toward the man who'd swept unexpectedly back into her life. "She's had a big day. I'll carry her into her room and tuck her in as soon as I finish washing the table."

"Why don't you take care of Lauryn, and I'll finish up here. Philip just sent me a text saying he'll be here in about five minutes."

Danielle nodded. The reprieve from the storm was over.

Ten minutes later, Jason was making introductions. "I appreciate your driving all the way here tonight, Philip."

"Sometimes face-to-face meetings beat a conference call, which is definitely the case right now. Besides, Garrett was a friend of mine, as well. I'm as determined as the two of you to ensure that whoever did this doesn't get away with it."

The IT specialist handed her his jacket. Beyond his *Lord of the Rings* T-shirt and the thick-framed glasses he wore, his fit physique carried no hint that he spent most of his time in front of a computer screen.

Funny the memories that popped up. While dating Jason, she'd gotten used to the self-proclaimed computer geeks he used to run around with. Date nights often ended with boxes of pizza and unending computer games while they spoke proudly about how their skills would one day change the world. She'd learned quickly that there was a lot more to them than just the stereotypical black-rimmed glasses and T-shirts with geek jokes.

"Can I get you anything?" Danielle hung up his jacket then shut the closet door. "We've got some lasagna left over from dinner."

"I'm fine, thanks. Picked up a burger and fries on the way here."

"How was the drive over?"

He smiled amiably. "Familiar. I think I've made that

drive a hundred times in the last couple years due to work."

Danielle took the seat beside Jason on the oversize couch, pulling her legs under her while Philip dragged his computer out of his bag across from them. Small talk seemed frivolous. There were things she needed to clarify in her mind before they went further.

"Before we get started, I know your company deals with security, but I would like to know what exactly was Garrett's job? With what I know about your company, I can't help but wonder if there could be a connection to all of what has happened and his work."

"You raise a very valid question." Philip looked up from his computer. "The security of our company is one of the reasons why we need to take this so seriously. Garrett, to put it simply, was a computer genius. He ran the computers side of the company with me while Jason focused on management."

"So he worked to ensure that your clients' online sensitive information was kept safe."

"Exactly. Data breaches can be not only costly, but with sensitive information—like credit card accounts, for example—security is essential." Philip pushed his glasses up. "We also do consulting on how to keep data safe among other things. Which is precisely why you're right. We have to look at the possibility that something Garrett did—whether intentional or not—might have compromised the integrity of our business."

"I asked Philip to look into specifically what Garrett had been working on over the past six months, and he came up with some interesting information." Jason leaned forward and rested his elbows against his knees. "One of the things we do is work on what we call information security which protects companies from losing information due to cyber attacks. Garrett was working on several accounts with companies that held classified government information."

Danielle realized that the picture they were painting was the perfect setup for what Garrett had experienced. "So while maybe what happened to Garrett had been nothing more than a romance scam, with murder now thrown into the mix, classified government information certainly would up the stakes."

"Yes. And there are other possibilities, as well," Philip threw out. "One of which is blackmail."

"How so?" Danielle asked.

"We call it industrial espionage," Jason explained. "Hackers frequently blackmail their victims by various means if their victim doesn't meet their demands."

"That sounds familiar." Too familiar.

"With the sensitive information Garrett dealt with on a daily basis, it's something we can't rule out."

"Here is what I don't understand." Danielle grabbed one of the mauve throw pillows from the couch beside her and hugged it to her chest as she worked to formulate her next question. "Why not simply come to one of you and confide what was going on? Why try to deal with this all on his own?"

"Garrett was very good at what he did," Jason said. "Admitting he was in some sort of trouble wouldn't have come easy for him. He might have tried to fix things himself, thinking in the end no one would be the wiser."

Danielle felt as if she was playing catch-up, but she had to admit it made sense. "In other words, how does a hacker admit he's been played?"

"Exactly. Garrett was a good guy, but essentially, he was still a hacker in the sense that his job was to find weaknesses in computer networks. When you're on the wrong side of the law, a hacker's job is to find his victim's weakness—not to become the victim himself."

"What about our hacker's identity?" Jason turned back to Philip. "Are we any closer to finding out who he is?"

"So far he's been able to hide his internet protocol address through different proxy servicers, which means we've been unable to pin down his identity."

Danielle shook her head. "Wait a minute. Protocol address and proxy servers don't mean anything to me."

Jason chuckled. "Basically, if you hide your public IP address by using an anonymous server your internet activity becomes difficult, if not impossible, to trace."

"Which means that with our hacker's abilities—along with information Garrett possessed," Philip added, "he could have found a way to hack into just about anything while avoiding getting caught."

There was one lingering question Danielle had to ask. "Do you think Garrett was clean?"

Jason looked at Philip. "It's something we can't dismiss, but we've both known Garrett for a very long time. I just can't imagine him betraying us or the company."

Philip shook his head. "I can't, either."

"Then what is the information Garrett had that our hacker now believes we have?" Danielle asked. "Clearly it was something believed to be worth Garrett's life."

"It could be a number of things." Philip set his laptop onto the couch beside him. "For starters, evidence of who was scammed and communicated with online. Stolen credit card numbers sold to other hackers…. The list could go on and on. I don't know about Jason, but I don't think we're looking at a typical hacker. Some simply steal identities, but this guy has taken things to the next level."

"I agree. Which could mean that Garrett had some

sort of intellectual property our hacker wanted, or some kind of leverage."

Danielle let out a slow breath. The questions were coming faster than the answers. "Leverage?"

"Shy of confronting him, which Garrett clearly did in the end, there's a method called doxing which is simply gathering information on someone using internet resources. Garrett would have been able to recognize information that would give him the advantage."

"So when Garrett met with our hacker, he came in thinking he had enough leverage on him to get what he wanted?" Danielle asked.

"That's what I think happened," Philip concurred. "He tried to turn the tables on our hacker. Garrett knew that identity theft will get you time in jail, but if he could prove our hacker was a threat to our national security, for example, then we're talking a whole different ball game."

"And there's a good chance that Garrett's death wasn't intentional." Jason added. "Because killing Garrett has put our hacker on the defensive."

Danielle fiddled with the fringe on the edges of the pillow, trying to process all the information they were doling out. "If you've found a way to steal government secrets worth millions—which evidently is an assumption regarding our hacker—why target me for simple identity fraud? Wouldn't my house loan seem like small change to him?"

Philip nodded. "Maybe what happened with Garrett was nothing more than a crime of opportunity, but on the other hand, it takes time to make your way up the ranks. In the meantime, our hacker did things to bring in a steady income while trying to stay under the radar."

"So what now?" Danielle asked. "The police are involved, but their time and resources are limited. The bank is doing their own investigation, as well, but that, too, is going to take time."

"I mentioned this earlier to Danielle." Jason said to Philip. "Up until this point, we've been on the defensive. Unable to do much more than play catch-up, and anticipating his next move is almost impossible, because he's in control."

"What are you thinking?" Philip asked, his eyes lighting with interest.

"That we're looking at things wrong. Our hacker has just killed a man which is more than likely out of the normal realm of how he functions. He's running scared, which means it's time we put *him* on the defensive."

"But how exactly would we do that?" Danielle asked.

Philip smiled. "We turn the tables on him."

TEN

"Turn the tables on our hacker? Isn't that what Garrett tried to do?" Danielle stood up and walked to the window before turning back to face Jason and Philip, her hands pressed against her hips. "Garrett tried to take the upper hand. All it did was end up getting him killed."

"That's true, but I still think we're on to something." Philip leaned forward, clearly in his element. "There are people who believe that if they can waste the time of these criminals, it gives the bad guys less time to actually take advantage of someone else."

"So we waste his time?" Danielle shook her head. "I don't get it."

"Basically, we promise him what he wants, *if* he gives us what we want."

Danielle sat back down by Jason still unconvinced. "You're talking about some kind of reverse blackmail?"

"You could call it that, I suppose."

"And if this ends up backfiring on us?"

"We deal with the fallout," Jason began, "when—and if—something like that happens."

A fallout in this case could prove deadly, but she knew exactly what she wanted from this guy. "I need him to not only leave me alone, but fix the damage he's already done.

The problem is, though, that we don't even have what he wants. What happens if he gives in to our demands then realizes the truth?"

"For now, the main advantage, besides undoing some of the damage he's done, is that it would buy us more time." Jason appeared to already be on board. "In the meantime, we'll have to pray that if he follows through on his end, that by then we have something to give him."

"I'm not willing to risk something happening to my daughter."

"Doing nothing is risking he'll strike again," Jason said. "What if there is a chance that we can reverse this mess? Philip might eventually be able to find this guy, but there's no telling how much damage he will have done by that time. The police are working the murder angle, but how long is it going to take for them to run their investigation? It's up to us."

"He's right, Danielle," Philip said. "We are out of time, and we've got to take the upper hand. We're not talking about confronting him in person like Garrett did. We're talking about playing his own game."

"If anything happens to Lauryn—"

"I'll do everything in my power to make sure she stays safe." Jason reached out and took her hand. "I promise, Danielle."

Danielle nodded, still feeling uneasy, but knowing she needed to trust him. "Then what do we do?"

Jason looked to Philip and nodded before turning back to Danielle. "We send him a message with a list of our demands."

Danielle pulled out the wooden hand-cranked coffee mill from the cupboard, poured in a scoop of beans and started grinding them. While cooking might not sit high on her list of talents, there was something therapeutic about grinding her own beans. She continued cranking the wheel, while the last hour and a half played over in her mind. They'd composed a message for the hacker, and in the end they'd emailed their own list of requisitions—including a deadline.

We'll give you forty-eight hours to meet our demands....

Worry gnawed at Danielle as she transferred the ground beans to the drip coffeemaker her mother had bought her last Christmas. After all, she couldn't rule out the possibility that they'd taken a risk that would backfire on them. What if their hacker's desperation didn't force him to meet their demands, but instead twisted the situation into something far worse?

Jason had tried to convince her that they were doing the right thing. That the possible benefits far outweighed the risks. All she could do was pray that they were right. The coffee began emitting the sweet scent of hazelnut into the room as Jason stepped into the kitchen a few minutes later.

"Smells fantastic," he said. "Looks as if you've got a few secrets up your sleeve."

"I try to make up for my lack of cooking skills with roasting and grinding my own beans."

She caught his gaze and tried to read his expression. Relaxed...intent...but there was also that familiar hint of interest in his vibrant blue eyes. A sense of longing she hadn't expected—or wanted—to see. No. She shoved the thought aside. Her nerves were just on edge.

When Philip had left to drive back home, she'd impulsively invited Jason to stay for coffee. She hadn't needed or even wanted the coffee—it had simply been an excuse for him to stay. Now she was wondering if she'd done the right thing.

She leaned back against the counter. "Did Philip get off okay?"

"Yeah."

"I appreciate his driving all this way," she murmured.

"Me, too. I think we came up with a viable solution."

Danielle pulled down two mugs from the cupboard. "You seem almost relaxed."

"I like to problem solve, and I feel as if we made progress tonight." He lifted a shoulder. "If nothing else we did something concrete."

Which was exactly what had her concerned. Engaging in a sparring match with a murderer probably meant someone was going to lose.

He tilted his head and caught her gaze. "But you, on the other hand, look worried."

She set the sugar bowl on the counter, then leaned back against the granite top. "I'm worried because this guy is smart. He didn't get to where he was because he flunked out of school. We both know that he's learned enough personal information to ruin me financially." She sighed. "Asking him to undo the damage assumes that he's willing to do anything to get this information."

She moved to the fridge to pull out the milk as the coffee finished percolating, still not completely convinced their plan would work.

"Listen," Jason continued. "I'll be the first to admit that what we did was a risk, but sitting back and doing nothing wasn't getting us anywhere, either. This creep's going to keep pushing until he gets what he wants."

"I'm just scared, Jason." She set two mugs on the counter, tired of the fear and frustration that were closing in around her. "Part of me knows we did the right thing, but

I can't help running all the scenarios through my mind about what might happen."

"Going over all of the *what-ifs* isn't going to change anything. And even if your fears come true…would it really have been worth doing nothing?"

She clenched her hands nervously. "Honestly, I don't know."

"Which is why it is a risk. All we can do is pray and go ahead with the plan." Jason grasped her hands, pulled them against his chest and bowed his head. "God, You know the fears we're facing and even more importantly, You already know the outcome. Give us the peace and wisdom we need today to face everything that is still ahead. Amen."

Danielle opened her eyes and let out a slow breath. "Thank you. I needed that."

She reached out to hand him one of the coffee mugs. When his fingers brushed against hers, Danielle felt her heart quicken. Confusion mingled with unwanted feelings of pent-up longing. The mug slipped from her hands, crashing against the kitchen floor. Hot coffee and shards of pottery splattered across the tiled floor between them.

Jason was the first to react. "Watch out. There's glass all over the floor."

"I'm sorry." Danielle let out a sharp breath and took a step backward.

"Are you burned?"

"I don't think so. Just a few splatters of coffee on my jeans that will come out in the wash. There is a dustpan right behind you."

Her hand was still shaking as she grabbed a roll of paper towels off the counter while he started picking up the broken mug and placing the shattered pieces into the dustpan.

A moment later, they stood up at the same time, close enough for her to note all the things about him she'd been trying to ignore…the color of his eyes, the curve of his smile, the slight curl of his hair. Everything about him was familiar.

He grasped the tips of her fingers. "Danielle, I know you're scared, but I meant what I said earlier. I promise I'm going to do everything in my power to keep you and Lauryn safe. I need you to trust me."

She started to pull away, but his arm slipped around her waist. He pulled her toward him. How did she explain that the pounding of her heart had nothing to do with an online criminal, or even the shattered coffee mug? Instead, it was the unexpected longing for something—for someone— she hadn't planned on waltzing back into her life.

But as much as she kept telling herself to resist, her heart knew this was exactly what she wanted. For a moment, she gave in to his kiss.

Jason hadn't intended to kiss Danielle, but standing beside her, feeling her heart pounding, had changed everything. Every excuse he'd come up with about guarding his heart vanished at the touch of her lips against his. It didn't matter that she'd once broken his heart with nothing more than a flimsy excuse. Didn't matter that he'd once vowed to forget about her.

All he knew was that the one woman he'd ever loved was right in front of him, and this time he had no intention of losing her again.

"Jason…" She pulled away before pressing the back of her hand against her lips.

He couldn't read her expression. "What's wrong?"

She took a step back, careful to avoid the glass. "I'm sorry. I can't do this."

"No, I'm sorry." He dropped his hands to his sides, wondering what he'd just done. "I had no right to take advantage of the situation. I don't know what came over me. I just…"

Except he did know. Although she'd shattered his trust, a part of him had never stopped loving her. Never stopped hoping that even after all these years something would bring them back together. And as much as he'd fought it, he'd spent his whole life comparing every girl he'd ever met to her, a habit that had been wrong. They were silly fantasies grounded in foolishness, but even that knowledge had never seemed to matter.

Danielle went back to cleaning up the glass. So much might have changed between them, but the need for her in his life still existed. As hard as he'd tried, that spark left dormant all these years still refused to die out.

Jason cleared his throat. As much as his heart wanted a second chance at their relationship, there were still certain things that needed to be said. "There are things we have to talk about. There were things left unresolved. Things I've never understood or been able to forget."

She dumped the dustpan full of glass into the trash can. The wall surrounding her heart was back up. "It's been a long time, Jason. Please don't tell me you never got over me…never got over us."

He could see the confusion in her eyes, but he wasn't ready to let her run this time. He deserved an explanation. Maybe with it he'd learn to forget the past and find someone else who might one day fill the void in his life.

"What really happened back then?" Now was as good a time as any to face the situation head-on. "I planned to spend the rest of my life with you. Maybe I wasn't the perfect catch, and yes, we were young, but I loved you.

I never would have hurt you on purpose, you have to believe me."

Danielle dropped the dustpan back into its place under the sink and turned to him. "Watching my father walk out on my mother changed me, making it harder for me to trust. And then there were things that happened the months leading up to our wedding. Things that made me wonder if I really could trust you with the rest of my life."

He leaned against the counter and folded his arms across his chest trying to read her expression. "What did I do to break your trust in me?"

"Looking back I don't know that it was ever anything you did. I loved you, too. You have to believe that. And I planned to marry you, have your babies and grow old together. But fear…fear can be a powerful motivator, and I didn't know how to tell you what I was really feeling…"

So she'd simply called off their wedding. Jason tried to sort through his own tangled web of feelings. They'd never been completely honest with each other back then. Which meant that they both had to start being honest now—no matter where things ended up between them.

"I'm not sure how to say this, because the past—our past—belongs there. I came to Pacific Cove to find my friend and business partner. Finding you here was totally unexpected." He took a deep, bolstering breath. "When you walked out of my life all of those years ago, you told me not to chase after you and I didn't. I wasn't then, nor am I now, looking for a second chance at love—" or being hurt again "—but the truth is that I'm as drawn to you now as the day we first met."

They'd taken the same art class their sophomore year. He'd tried to blow it off, like he had with most of his classes, while she'd soaked up everything there was to learn. Somehow they'd found truth in the saying that opposites attract. He'd been the class clown; she'd been the studious one with good grades. He loved slamming dunks on the basketball courts; she'd preferred an afternoon at the museum. Somehow she'd fallen for him, captured his heart, and his life had never been the same again.

Losing her had left a gap that he'd never been able to fill. And all these years later, he still managed to avoid commitment.

"You can't tell me you don't feel the same way?"

Danielle rubbed her fingers against her temple. "I'd be lying if I said I didn't feel something, but I don't know that I can deal with this right now."

Jason realized if he wasn't careful, he'd end up pushing her away. She'd loved and lost which made her heart vulnerable. But he'd also loved and lost. And while finding her again hadn't been a part of his plan, how could he simply let her go? Kissing her had only proven that his heart still felt.

"I'm not asking you for anything other than your honesty," he continued. "Because even I don't know if I'm ready for anything more than that. I'm just asking you to keep your mind—and heart—open and don't push me away."

"I just… I can't do this right now. I'm sorry."

He shook his head, wondering what he had been thinking. She'd been right all along. Those lost years between them were too much to circumnavigate. Just because Garrett's murder had thrust them together didn't mean he could expect her to feel the same way he did right now.

"I guess I should go."

She nodded then turned away without saying anything else.

Jason slipped out the front door and was gone.

ELEVEN

Danielle watched the red glow of her bedside clock switch from 4:29 to 4:30 a.m. Lightning flashed in a zig-zag pattern behind the heavy drapes covering her window. Last night's predicted storm had finally hit, bringing with it driving rains and howling winds. She rolled over, drawing the pile of blankets with her, surprised Lauryn hadn't woken up to join her in the queen-size bed.

She, on the other hand, had been awake the past hour, her thoughts alternating between desperate prayers for wisdom and peace to futile attempts to shut off her mind so she could fall back to sleep. Instead, she'd fought to suppress one frightening scenario after another. Her father had always told her to look the worst-case scenario in the eye and face it—but in this case the worst meant losing everything she'd worked for.

She wasn't sure she could face that outcome.

Thunder crackled in the distance, stirring up memories of storm watching with her father while waves crashed against steep cliffs and rocks jutting out of the Pacific's swirling waters. They'd hunkered down in seaside cafés or restored lighthouses and studied the ever-changing mood of the Pacific. Until her father had left for another woman and never returned.

Which was one reason her hacker wasn't the only thing bothering her tonight.

On top of everything else there was Jason who had stepped back into the picture and managed to find a hole in her normally well-fortressed heart. She'd never meant to hurt him all those years ago, and she'd never meant to hurt him last night, either. But neither was she willing to jump into a relationship when her emotions were already in a jumbled mess. His kiss might have proven that she still had feelings for him, but her need for support wasn't the same as her need for love. And mixing the two would only get them both into trouble.

She ran the back of her hand across her mouth. She had no idea what category to fit Jason into. College sweetheart? Hero? Heartbreaker?

In a sense, Jason Ryan had been all those things—until she'd given him up for a stint in Europe. And while she might still harbor regrets over their breakup, even she had to admit her surprise in discovering dormant feelings for the man she'd once promised to marry.

Danielle dismissed the thought as she threw off the covers, and hurried across the carpeted floor toward the shower. She shivered in the cold outside her electric blanket. Neither of them were the same person they'd been back in college. Her past nostalgia had simply been intensified by the explosive situation they'd been thrust into together. If they'd met on the street, they'd have said hello, caught up politely on friends and family then went their separate ways. She didn't owe him anything, nor should she feel guilt over what happened between them.

Except none of that was exactly true, either. She turned on the hot water and grabbed a thick towel from the cabinet, wishing she could erase the lingering threads of betrayal to Quinton…and the long-forgotten question of what would have happened if she'd chosen to marry Jason.

Her phone dinged with an email message, from where she'd left it last night on the bathroom counter. Her breathing slowed as she thumbed through the messages and junk mail that had come through overnight, while the hot water steamed up the mirror in front of her. But there was no response from their hacker. No indication at all that he'd received their ultimatum.

They'd baited him, but until he responded, she'd simply have to wait. The game wasn't over.

Forty-five minutes later, she turned in to the parking lot of The Bamboo Closet earlier than normal after dropping off a sleepy Lauryn at her mother's, thankful her mom was always up before the sun rose. Pulling into an empty space, she grabbed her handbag and keys and exited the car while trying to open her umbrella. A gust of wind caught the edge of the waterproof fabric as she braced herself against the pouring rain and rushed toward the front of the building.

Her hand trembled as she unlocked the door of the shop, the shaking as much from the circumstances she found herself in, as from the morning cold. Dropping the wet umbrella into the round metal bin, she automatically locked the door behind her. She might feel paranoid, but with all that had happened, being careful seemed prudent.

Running her fingers through her damp hair, she tried to pretend that today was just like any other day in her weekly routine. Drop Lauryn at her mother's at seven for the day, open up the store, spend a few quiet minutes reading her Bible, ensure the store was ready for a new set of customers…. She loved the early mornings before her employees arrived. It had taken years of hard work to establish her business, along with the need for continued marketing and sales strategies. But all the sweat and tears had been worth it.

Doing it all on her own after Quinton's death had been a challenge, but losing him had forced her to adapt. Knowing she had to provide for her daughter had kept her going. She'd learned to handle the employees, deal with customers, keep up with the accounting, while still doing all the buying for the store.

Danielle flipped on the light switch at the entrance. Nothing. She flipped it again, then sighed. She'd have to call the electrician. It wasn't the first time she'd had trouble with the electricity, but Kate and Sarah would arrive within the hour and customers after that. Which meant besides getting the lights back on, she needed her daily caffeine jolt to get her moving.

The dim glow from the outside streetlight was enough for her to make her way toward the small employee room at the back of the store. Halfway across the showroom floor, she froze when she heard the familiar squeak of the wooden floor in the back corner. Someone was in the building.

No. She forced herself to take a calming breath. She was only imagining things. The past forty-eight hours had managed to put a boogeyman around every corner.

Danielle leaned into the shadow of an antique French armoire and listened. One of the last things she'd asked Quinton to do was replace the warped board. He'd died before he'd had a chance to fix it, and she'd never made it a priority. The old shop had its quirks, but she'd always loved the quaint, seaside building with its rustic exterior and aged wood floors inside.

The floor squeaked again.

This time she knew she'd heard something. Someone *was* in the store.

Danielle moved quietly toward the back wall of the showroom lined with chunky framed mirrors and unique artwork collections. She reached for her phone in her jacket pocket, but came up empty. She frowned, trying to remember where she'd left it. She'd called her mom on the way to see if Lauryn had gone back to sleep. She had to have left it in her car.

During the day, the cluttered arrangement of the shop worked with the eclectic mixture. In the darkness, though, the yellow glow of the streetlights hanging outside the store simply cast eerie shadows along the wall. But she knew the store layout, which gave her the advantage in the darkened space.

She made her way silently through tall wooden shelves of pottery and glassware, candlesticks and heavy wooden chests. She stopped again, searching for movement, anything that would give away his position in the darkness. She drew in a deep breath and prayed for clarity. Quinton had insisted on putting in an alarm system. All she had to do was get to the panel and punch in the panic code.

She caught movement among the shadows.

Danielle grabbed a metal candlestick from the display behind her and slowly raised it above her head. She'd trained for three triathlons over the past five years, but knew little about self-defense. She leaned farther back as another thought emerged. What if the intruder was her hacker? A cold shiver ran down her spine. He'd murdered Garrett…and had a gun.

If he was desperate, as they believed, he might not hesitate to make her his next victim.

Danielle crouched beside a glass table and reached up to grab the back of one of the padded chairs with her free hand for balance. She studied the shadows on the wall, searching for a way out. Shades of yellow and gray flickered in the dim light. She caught sight of a silhouette coming around the corner. She squinted, trying to make out his features, but all she could see was a hooded figure about her height. He'd just blocked off her route to the security panel in the back. Taking the time to unlock the front door would make her the perfect target.

She pressed her lips together. *God, I need a way out of here....*

On the table beside her was a bowl of decorative spheres. She gripped one between her fingers, then threw it as hard as she could. The sphere smashed into a mirror near the back door.

The intruder rushed toward the noise.

Danielle ran toward the key pad and punched in the distress code. Seconds later, the shriek of a siren filled the room.

Jason pulled into one of the open parking spaces in front of The Bamboo Closet. Despite what had happened between them last night, he never should have left her alone. At a minimum, he should have insisted she spend the night at her mother's, then he could have picked her up this morning and driven her to work.

He'd stayed up half the night, working with Philip. They'd scoured Garrett's financial records and did full background checks of her employees, looking for anything they might have missed that would in turn lead to Garrett. But everything they'd studied came up empty. He'd finally fallen asleep about two o'clock, only to be awakened by Danielle's frantic phone call a few hours later.

All he knew was that someone had broken into the shop, and Danielle had sounded scared and vulnerable. Somehow, they had to find a way for this to end.

She sat in the middle of the showroom on a square leather ottoman staring off into the distance while someone from the security company asked her questions. There were dark shadows beneath her eyes. If she'd slept at all last night, she hadn't slept well.

He waited until the man left. She looked up at him, her gaze a mixture of raw emotion and determination. "Thanks for coming."

"Of course." He hesitated for a moment then sat across from her on a teal ottoman with pink flowers on top. "What happened?"

She crossed her arms over her knees and continued staring off into the distance. "Someone was in the store when I showed up."

"Are you okay?"

"I was able to avoid a confrontation, though maybe I shouldn't have. If it was the hacker, at least we'd know who we were dealing with. I don't even have a decent description beyond the shape of his shadow in the darkness."

"You think it could have been the hacker?"

She shrugged, then let the air seep slowly from her lungs. "Without more evidence, the police want to treat it like a typical break-in, because a couple hundred dollars is missing from the cash box."

"All that matters at this point is that you're okay." He leaned forward, wishing he could reach out and grasp her hands, yet respecting her need to keep her distance. Instead, he folded his hands together in his lap. "What about your alarm system? Did it go off?"

"I was able to punch in the panic code. The siren went off, and he escaped through a window in the back, running away on foot. I've just spoken to the security company and need to answer some more questions for the police who said they'd talk to me again in a few minutes.

As soon as everyone is gone, they want me to take an inventory to see if anything else was taken."

"What can I do?" he asked.

"Exactly what you are doing. Showing up at the crack of dawn, sitting here with me and reminding me that I'm not going crazy." She looked up at him with those big eyes of hers. He understood the internal battle raging inside when you felt that everything in your world was out of control. "Especially when I practically kicked you out of my house last night."

He cleared his throat. "This might not be the time, but…" It was a subject he'd rather avoid, but knew he couldn't. "I owe you an apology for last night."

"Forget it. I think we've both done enough apologizing over the past few days to make it even between us." She shot him a weak smile. "I just… I wasn't expecting you to show up in my life again, and then with the kiss… It's been a tough week. Everything that has happened has managed to play with our emotions."

Which was something else he'd realized. He'd been foolish to think that any emotion either of them felt was anything more than a result of the situation they'd both been thrust into. Because she was correct. Tense circumstances had a way of toying with one's emotions. Which meant that any feelings he thought he still had could easily be little more than his heart's wishful thinking. It was time he let her go.

At least that is what he was trying to convince himself.

"You have to believe that kissing you was never on my agenda. It just…it just happened."

He might have known that kissing her had been a mistake, but deep down he didn't regret it. Even if kissing Danielle had only made him want to be with her more.

"We need to figure this out together," she began, "but

I'm not ready to pick up where we left off, or if I'm even able to think about something beyond friendship between us. I'm not sure I'll ever be able to do that again. You have to understand."

He saw the hesitation in her eyes, along with the fear and vulnerability. He felt the same things, but the problem was that they had a bigger problem to figure out right now. Maybe when all this was over and life got back to normal...

"Mrs. Corbett?"

Danielle looked up at the officer.

"We are going to need a description of the person who broke into your store before we leave."

"I'm sorry, but like I told the other officer, I didn't get a good look at him. All I know is that he was about my height, maybe an inch taller, and a bit wiry."

"Hair color? Anything that might help with the description."

She shook her head. "It was still dark, and he was wearing some kind of hood that covered his head."

"If there's nothing else, then as soon as you've done a full inventory to see if anything was taken, you'll need to turn in an official report." The officer dropped his pen into his front pocket. "I understand that Detective Rodriguez is the officer working another case you're involved in concerning identity theft?"

"Yes. We spoke to him yesterday."

"I'll be in communication with him, and we will discuss further about the possibilities that the two cases are connected. In the meantime, I would advise you to change security codes and passwords."

Jason felt the guilt fester, wondering what he'd done. All their attempts to turn the tables on their hacker had only made him believe she had Garrett's evidence. And possibly put her life in danger.

Danielle stared at the shattered window in the back room of the store. Besides searching the place, she was going to have to have the window replaced. Which would take both time and money.

"After my initial walk-through of the store, it's hard to know what to look for," she began.

Jason glanced over her. "There is always the possibility that whoever broke in dropped something that the police missed."

"I suppose anything's possible at this point." She followed him into her office, which seemed the most logical place to start. Like her showroom inventory, she'd filled the space with an eclectic mixture of furniture and accent pieces she'd picked up over the years on her buying trips. Wooden storage cabinets with wicker baskets, a zebra-print storage bench under the window and her favorite—a funky wooden desk she'd decoupaged with vintage postcards.

But the normally neat office space was now a mess. The file cabinet had been ransacked, papers sifted through, drawers and cupboards lining the back wall left open. She'd clearly caught the intruder on his way out after most of the damage was done.

They worked in silence. Danielle sorted through files and paperwork while Jason did his best to help organize the mess. After an hour, the rain had finally stopped, and the sun was peeking through the line of clouds.

Jason stood up and stretched his back. "Anything?"

She shook her head. "Far as I can see nothing is missing."

He took a step backward and tipped over the metal

garbage can beside the desk. He started to pick up the mess then stopped. "When is the last time the trash was taken out?"

Danielle looked up at him. "I have professional cleaners come in every Saturday night. The staff is supposed to take out the trash during the week, but if we're busy it doesn't always get done."

"So how many days?"

"I don't know. Beginning of the week, more than likely. Why?"

He pulled out an orange wrapper. "This is a Zotz Fizz candy wrapper."

She shot him a blank stare. "I have customers coming through here all the time, and you wouldn't believe all the gum and wrappers they leave. Half the time they don't even make it into a trash can."

"I'm sure that is true, but one, this is your office where I assume most customers never see. And two, do you know what this is?"

She shook her head, still not getting his point. "A candy wrapper of some kind."

"Garrett's favorite candy he ordered online by the box. He had this crazy habit of keeping a stash in his pocket while he worked."

Danielle frowned. "Are you trying to tell me you think Garrett was here in my office?"

"That's exactly what I'm saying. This can't be another coincidence, Danielle. Garrett was here in your store."

TWELVE

Danielle fingered the empty candy wrapper. She'd never liked solving puzzles with missing pieces. Growing up, her mother had spent hours working on them on the card table in the living room. But instead of relaxing, Danielle had always found them frustrating. Hunting for matching colors, searching for the right pieces… Somehow, there always seemed to be a piece missing.

Today had proven to be exactly the same. Everything that had happened over the past few days had left her with unanswered questions and a growing frustration she didn't know how to resolve.

She dropped the wrapper back onto the desk and looked up at Jason. "Let's work through this. Why would Garrett come here?"

"The more I think about Garrett coming here, the more it makes sense, actually. Not only was he here in Pacific Cove. He called you. When you hung up on him, maybe he thought he could make you believe him if you talked to him face-to-face."

The reasoning didn't add up. "If he was looking for me, he didn't try very hard. I'm here most of the time, and even if I was out, there is always an employee who could pass along a message."

"Maybe someone didn't want you to know he was here?"

"Again why? I'm not ready to simply blow off your theory, but he's clearly not the only person who eats this particular candy."

"You're right, but considering the situation, I still don't think we can simply chalk it up as a coincidence."

"Maybe there is a way to know for sure." Danielle hurried over to the laptop sitting on her desk and sat down in her office chair. "I still need to go through the footage from this morning's break-in, but if we can find Garrett on the security footage, as well, we might be able to see who he spoke to."

Danielle logged into her security account and her inbox, hoping they'd finally found their first real break.

"How long are your videos accessible?"

She clicked onher inbox. "Fourteen days. Longer if there is footage I want to save. Otherwise everything is automatically overwritten."

"Which means that there is a chance that if he was here, we will still be able to access the video he was on."

"And today's intruder, as well." Danielle clicked through the screens, then stopped.

"Jason…"

He leaned over, resting his elbows against the edge of her desk. "What's wrong?"

"They're gone. All of them." She tried refreshing the page, with no luck. "Every bit of footage from the past two weeks has been erased."

"Let me take a look."

She moved out of the way so he could sit in the chair in front of the computer, then shoved back a strand of hair from her face. "This is impossible."

"Apparently not, because you're right. There is nothing in the trash folder, nothing in storage…it's all been wiped out."

Temples throbbing, she pressed her palm against her forehead, wanting to scream. "How could this have happened? To erase security footage from the hard drive you have to enter a code. It's supposed to be a security system, completely inaccessible to anyone else."

"Who has the passwords to access the system?"

"No one." She shook her head, trying to think how someone could have done this. "I thought it was safer that way."

"Where do you keep your passwords?"

"I have so many to keep track of…" She unlocked the top drawer of her desk and pulled out a small notebook. "I keep them in here, but everything is written in code so even if someone finds the book, they wouldn't be able to figure out the codes. At least that's what I thought."

Danielle sat against the edge of her desk. Either she'd been careless, allowing someone to figure out her password, or the hacker had found a way to access her video surveillance.

Jason leaned back and thumbed through the book. "At this point, it looks as if the footage was erased for one of two reasons. Either Garrett's visit, or this morning's break-in."

"Or both, if it is our hacker. Though I'm assuming he would have had the ability to erase the footage without being in the store." She looked up at Jason. "If he could transfer money from my home equity loan, finding out my employee record would have been easy. Just like hacking into my security system and erasing any record that he had been here."

"You have a point." He tapped his fingers against the desk. "Your surveillance system works from IP-based cameras that enable you to view the footage from a remote location, right?"

"Correct."

"Which means if you know what you are doing, it is possible to erase the files remotely," he explained.

"But there isn't any way to know for sure what he wanted off these tapes." She closed eyes, her mind spinning at all the possibilities. If he could hack into her security system, he wouldn't need an inside person. He'd clearly done enough damage on his own. But then what was on those surveillance cameras he—or someone else—didn't want her to see?

"We can start by showing a photo of Garrett to Kate and Sarah," she proposed. "If he was here, video footage or not, someone had to have seen something."

"I'm sure I've got a photo somewhere." Jason thumbed through his iPhone for a minute, then held up a photo for her to look at. "This was taken last Christmas at a ski trip up in Colorado, but if you ask me, Garrett looks about the same as he did in college."

"Good. Let's just hope it will work."

Jason pushed the chair away from the desk and stood up. "By the way, Philip has looked at all your current employees, but what about past employees? Are there any that might hold a grudge? Someone you fired, or someone who would know how the shop works and have reason to try and gain access?"

Danielle worked backward mentally through the past few months. "There was…a guy. His name was Marty Devonport. He started working part-time for me this past summer. I ended up firing him after finding out he'd stolen a couple hundred dollars out of the cash drawer." She hesitated. "He was angry—more at getting caught than losing his job—but he left without causing a scene in the end."

Her phone dinged as an email came through, momentarily distracting her from the conversation. Her heart pounded as she scrolled through the recent messages.

Jason put down his phone and turned back to her. "Anything?"

"A sale on chicken wings, but nothing from our hacker yet."

"Give him time," he said. "The hacker's probably weighing his response."

She flipped the phone shut and shoved it into her back pocket. "And if we ended up pushing him too hard?"

"Let's not take on that problem unless we have to."

Danielle crossed her arms, still worried that taking things into their own hands hadn't been a move in the right direction. What were the chances he was simply going to give them what they'd wanted because they asked nicely? "Danielle…?"

She looked up at him, grateful for his nearness as the conflicting battle between trust and fear raged within her. "I'm sorry. I just can't stop thinking about when this is going to stop. I feel as if I'm playing some game of cat and mouse, but I'm always one step behind no matter what we do. I don't know how much longer I can keep this up and time is running out. What's he going to do next?"

"I don't know." Jason's eyes reflected his frustration. "None of us do."

"Which is the problem. I can't be proactive in a situation when I don't know where the next strike is coming from. How do I protect my business and Lauryn when I don't know the rules of the game?"

She took a deep breath, trying to find a sliver of peace to hold on to. "I hate it when my faith wavers, but I guess

I thought God would have already stepped in and stopped this. And now that He hasn't—not yet, anyway—I'm just not sure where He is or how much strength I'm going to need to get through this."

They both knew that the storm was far from over. And how somehow—even in facing the possibility of losing everything—she needed something tangible to hold on to.

"I certainly don't have all the answers, but I do know that He's right here in the middle of all of this, Danielle. Sometimes He doesn't calm the storm around us, but He always gives us what we need to get through it." He locked eyes with her as he gently took her hand in his. "When I lost my mom, I don't think I'd ever felt so alone. Funny how at that moment, everyone had a verse or some platitude that was supposed to make me feel better, when half the time what was said only made me feel worse."

Swallowing a lump in her throat, she nodded. She'd been there before. That place of pure rawness where nothing anyone says seems to make a difference. All she knew to do was hold on to her faith and keep trusting until the storm subsided no matter how hard the waves hit. And Jason had become a part of her shelter in this storm.

"Looking back," he continued, "I can see God's fingerprints were everywhere. I know it sounds like a formulated answer, and that's not what I'm going for here, but what I do know is that He is here, and He cares what happens to you in this situation."

She nodded again, thankful that he didn't automatically throw out a bunch of pat answers. Because she knew all the *right* answers. Knew God was right here in the midst of the storm…. And although her faith faltered at times, deep down she knew Jason was right. In the end, she'd seen God's hand working, and in relying on Him, she'd become a stronger person. It was hard to see those truths in the eye of the storm.

She slid down off the side of the desk, needing something that would both pick up her mood and boost her energy level.

"Where are you going?" he asked.

"I don't know about you, but I never got my cup of coffee this morning."

Jason watched Danielle walk out of the office and decided to stay put in order to give her some space. All her points were valid. It was impossible to be in control of a situation when you had no idea what the next move was going to be. He ran his hand across the back of his neck. There had to be a way to end all of this.

He moved near the large window that overlooked an empty lot, pulled out his phone and punched in Philip's number. Knickknacks from different places she'd visited around the world sat neatly on shelves beside an assortment of art, travel and design books. On the walls, she'd hung framed photos of Rome, Paris and Morocco.

The photo that caught his eye, though, was one of her with a little girl from Mexico. She stood beside Danielle wearing a tattered shirt, flip-flops and a broad smile. A small sign at the bottom stated that a percentage of the profits from The Bamboo Closet went to help orphans like Maria.

Jason smiled. Danielle might question her beliefs sometimes, but she'd clearly found ways to live out her faith. He turned back to the window. Part of him felt like an intruder. Everywhere he looked were her personal touches, giving him further insight into who she'd become. And the more he saw, the more he felt the strong temptation to move their relationship forward.

Jason was about to hang up when Philip finally picked up. "Hey. Just wanted to let you know that there was a break-in at Danielle's store early this morning."

"Was anything taken?"

"Her office was gone through, but the only thing she found missing was some petty cash. The strange thing is that her surveillance footage was erased."

"Why would someone do that?" Philip asked.

"That's what we are both wondering."

There was a short pause on the line. "I've got a guy who specializes in recovering data. I'll give him a call and see what he can do."

"That would be great. Thanks."

Even if Philip could recover some of the video, it could still end up being another dead end, but at least he was doing something.

"I've also got the name of a past employee that might be holding a grudge against Danielle." Jason passed on the man's name. "I think it's worth looking into his record, as well."

"While you've got me on the phone, I was actually getting ready to call you," Philip said. "I've come up with something else interesting. I was able to match a user name on Danielle's email server to an online dating service we found on Garrett's computer. Now it could be nothing more than a coincidence…"

Jason shook his head. "I'm not buying anything as coincidence at this point."

"I'd say you're right on that count."

"Have you got a real name?" Jason asked.

"Not yet. Unfortunately, most people use a tag name or a moniker on these dating sites. People are encouraged to guard their anonymity by not using any identifying information online for safety issues, but in situations like this it makes it hard to investigate. And on top of that, she'd just deleted her profile. But I'll keep working on tracking her down."

A moment after Jason hung up, Danielle came back into the office holding two mugs of coffee. He reached for the one she handed him and took a sip. "Thanks. Better?"

She sat down on her purple swivel desk chair, setting her mug in front of her. "As long as I can keep the coffee coming along with keeping things in perspective, I just might make it."

"Here's something new to add to the fire. I just got off the phone with Philip. You might have been right about Garrett. He might not have been here to see you."

Danielle shook her head. "Then why was he here?"

"Philip told me he was able to match the user name off Garrett's computer to one on your server, connecting them both to an online dating service."

"Wow. That means Garrett was possibly dating one of my employees?"

Jason nodded. "Which could explain why the tapes were erased. Maybe whoever it was didn't want you to know about their relationship."

"So now there's a chance that whoever Garrett was dating has no connection to our hacker. This is becoming a tangled web that I don't know how to unravel."

Jason took another sip of his coffee that wasn't quite up to the quality of her freshly ground brew. "Do you know what my grandmother used to say when I complained about life getting too tangled?"

There was a hint of a smile in her eyes. "Do I want to know?"

"Go buy another skein of yarn."

"Very funny." Danielle tapped on the side of the mug with her fingernail. "In all seriousness, though, I'm not sure I know how to start over. But I do appreciate your help." Her gaze dropped. "I don't know what I would have done without your being here."

"I'm just sorry you're having to go through all of this in the first place. And as for me…I've said it before. I need resolution as much as you do."

She looked up and caught his gaze, her eyes full of emotion. His desire to take care of her and ensure she was safe deepened…along with his reawakened feelings toward her. He leaned toward her until he was close enough to catch the subtle scent of strawberries in her hair. Until he was close enough to kiss her. This time she didn't pull away.

The bell on the front door jingled. Jason stepped back at the interruption. There was still so much left unsaid between them. But all of that was going to have to wait for another day.

Danielle walked toward the front of the store as Kate and Sarah stepped into the building off the boardwalk. She'd always taken pride in living in a town where the worst crimes were typically limited to petty theft and underage drinking on the beach. Now it seemed as if everything had changed with Garrett's murder. Most of all, she hated her initial reaction of suspicion toward those she considered to be her friends, but she didn't know how to turn it off. Garrett had been dating someone who had access to her computers.

Which as far as she could see narrowed it down to someone who worked for her.

"Danielle." Kate dropped her gym bag onto the floor beside her. Her shoulder-length, curly brown hair had been tied back for her morning workout. She fingered a pearl pendant hanging from a silver chain. "What's going on? Caroline from next door just told us that the store was broken into."

"There was a break-in. I was here when—"

"You were here?" Sarah pressed her hand against her mouth in horror.

"The intruder escaped."

"Thank God." Kate's expression darkened as she looked around the room. "Was anything stolen?"

"He trashed my office, but far as I know, only the petty cash was taken."

"I'm so sorry. I can't even imagine how terrified I would have been." Sarah wrapped her arm around Danielle's shoulder. "What can we do?"

"Honestly, I don't know." She shook her head. If one of her employees were involved, it would seem that the less they knew about what they were doing to find out the truth, the better.

She made a quick introduction of Jason who'd just joined them.

"Kate. Sarah. This is Jason. He's an expert with securities and is helping me. Besides that, I'm sure that the police will want to speak to each of you, as well, at some point."

Kate shook her head. "Who do you think could have done this?"

"I don't know that, either." Which was true. Danielle still wasn't totally buying into the idea that one of her employees had betrayed her.

Danielle looked at her friends. Sarah worked to put herself through night school, planned to be a massage therapist and dabbled with crocheted items she sold on eBay. She lived in an apartment near the coast, wore vintage clothes and loved playing beach volleyball.

She'd known Kate for years. Running the shop had

come naturally to her friend, which was why over the years Danielle had given Kate more and more responsibility. No red flags. No arrests or jail time. But wasn't that the point of a cyber hacker—working like a chameleon appearing to be something they weren't?

"What about Rae?" Sarah slipped off her lime-green coat and slung it over her arm. "Kate and I were just talking this morning about how she's never been back to work. We've both tried to call her, but she doesn't answer her phones. We still have her last paycheck."

"I've told the police that the timing of her quitting seems strange."

"Here's another angle." Jason pulled out his phone and clicked on his photo of Garrett. "Have either of you seen this man?"

Sarah took the phone and studied the photo. "Who is he?"

"He's a friend of mine. We think he stopped by the store a few days ago, possibly to talk to Danielle."

Sarah passed the phone to Kate. "I don't know him."

"Me neither." Kate shook her head then handed the phone back to Jason. "So what next, Danielle? Do you plan to open the store today?"

"I don't know." Danielle looked to Jason. "I need to file a police report, change my security codes, finish putting my office back together, arrange to have the back window fixed…"

Running a business was complicated on a good day. With everything else she needed to deal with, closing the shop for a few days wasn't an unreasonable option. But she wasn't the only one the loss of income was going to effect.

"You have enough to deal with," Sarah began. "Kate and I can manage the store."

"She's right, Danielle," Kate said. "There's no use losing business."

"Okay." Danielle nodded, realizing they were right. "I appreciate you both for coming through for me."

A minute later, she and Jason were back in her office. He shut the door behind him. "Do you trust them?"

Danielle grappled with the question. "I've never had reason not to. I wouldn't have been able to do what I do without either of them over the past couple of years."

"Who else then? If it's not one of them, or Rae, then who?"

Danielle's phone went off. It was another email. She glanced at the return address and felt her stomach roil. "It's him, Jason."

"Maybe he's finally decided to give in to our demands."

She scrolled down the email.

"They're photos, Jason. Photos... of me dropping off Lauryn at my mother's..."

No place was safe. He knew where she lived, where she worked. He knew how to get to Lauryn.

THIRTEEN

Danielle couldn't breathe. Everything she'd done to protect her daughter had just shattered into a million worthless pieces. She grabbed her bag from the top of her desk and started rummaging for her car keys. What had possessed her to gamble over her child's life? She couldn't change what had happened, but she could get her daughter and mother somewhere safe for the three of them to stay until this guy was found and locked away for the rest of his life. They could drive south…disappear—

"Danielle, where are you going?" Jason's voice rippled through her, yanking her out of her numbing thoughts.

"I've got to get Lauryn somewhere safe."

She rushed toward the front of the store, ignoring the questioning looks of Kate and Sarah. She wasn't in the mood for an argument. Not when she'd been thrust once again into the eye of the storm. Outside, she opened up the car door and found her phone where she'd left it on the console.

I know You're here, God, but I just can't feel Your presence in the middle of all of this…. I need something… something tangible that shows me You're here.

Jason was right behind her. "We will get Lauryn somewhere safe, but you've got to think this through before you rush off without a plan."

"What we did might have been a calculated risk, but it wasn't supposed to come to this." She turned to face him. "He's a computer hacker. He's supposed to stick to computer hacking, not threats against my family."

"You're right. What we did was a risk that might have backfired, but that doesn't mean that this is over, or that we're just going to give up." Jason grasped her shoulders, but she pulled away. "You've got to think through this."

"You have a better idea at this point?"

Danielle turned away with her phone. He didn't deserve her theatrics, but she couldn't let this guy win. Her fingers fumbled to press the correct buttons on her phone. An eternity passed until her mother picked up.

"Mom, it's me. I need you to do exactly what I say. Pack a suitcase for the next few days and throw in some of Lauryn's things you keep there at your house. I'll be there in the next ten minutes."

"Danielle—"

"I need you to make sure the doors are locked and don't answer it for anyone except me." She stared down the boardwalk at the familiar row of cafés, hotels and shops. A couple walked hand in hand, pausing to look in one of the windows. Decorations were being hung for this weekend's Seafood Festival… "Mom, do you understand?"

"No, I don't. What's going on?"

She should have told her mom what was happening. Shouldn't have thought she could handle things alone. "It's too long to explain right now, but the man I tried to save on the beach was Jason's best friend. Apparently he'd been scammed by a con artist. Now this guy's hacked into my financial accounts, and I'm worried…I'm worried he knows how to get to Lauryn."

Saying it out loud made her feel as if she were crazy.

"Danielle? How could you not have told me?"

"I'm sorry, Mom. I promise I'll explain more later, but for now, I just need you to trust me."

She hung up the phone and started to get into the car.

"Stop for a minute, Danielle." He pulled her toward him, his hands pressed gently against her shoulders. This time he didn't let her move away from him. She felt her body tense at his nearness. Wanting him to hold her as much as she wanted to run.

"He's playing with you. Trying to get in your head."

"Then he's succeeded." Her eyes filled with tears. "He killed your best friend. Don't tell me that his next move is limited to some stupid financial hacking. He knows how to get what he wants. He's going after Lauryn."

"Danielle, you're not driving anywhere."

"I have to get my daughter. Clearly we're not safe and any leverage we thought we had doesn't faze him."

"Give me the keys. I'll drive you."

"I'm fine driving—"

"Danielle, forget everything that was between us and all the scenarios running through your head right now. Let me help you."

Anger toward him dissipated. She needed somewhere tangible to place her frustration. She didn't know what to do. Didn't know how to make this okay again. But maybe God had sent her what she needed for the moment. "I need to be with my daughter. I need to make sure that she is safe."

"I understand, but we also need a plan. Let me help you do this."

She felt her shoulders relax slightly. "Our last plan only ended up antagonizing the hacker. My plan is to make sure that my daughter is as far away as possible.

You asked me what I needed earlier. I need this to end. I need to know that my daughter is safe when I leave her for the day at my mom's." Tears clogged her throat. "I need to know that my bank account isn't going to be drained when I wake up in the morning, or that some crazed hacker hasn't spent half my retirement and put me out of business."

She leaned against the side of the car, struggling to breathe, and hating that she couldn't stop sobbing. "I don't know how to deal with this, except to take my family as far away from here as possible."

"Then let's start there. Where do you want to go?"

"I don't know."

He grabbed her hand that held keys dangling from her fingers and squeezed gently. "There is a good chance that his threats aren't as solid as he wants us to think they are. I don't think for an instant that he's won yet. He still wants whatever Garrett had, which is our one trump card."

"Maybe you're right, but I can't just sit around and do nothing while my child's life is threatened."

A look of fierce determination crossed his face. "We're not going to sit around and do nothing, but you don't need to be driving right now."

"Jason, I—" His other hand moved to push back the hair the wind had blown against her cheek. She sucked in a breath and tried to stop the waves of fear threatening to take hold. He was right. She was in no condition to drive. Her hands shook as she gave him the keys. She needed to draw on what they had just spoken about last night, because nothing had really changed. God was here, right here in the midst of everything. But while she believed that, walking by faith still wasn't always easy.

She looked up at him, trying to fight the desperation

closing in on her. "Promise me nothing will happen to Lauryn."

"I promise that I will do everything in my power to protect you and your daughter."

She nodded, knowing that what she asked was unreasonable. There were no guarantees in life. She of all people knew that. And she couldn't let the fear paralyze her.

She'd seen it once when her mother's house had been broken into while her mother had been sleeping. The police had told them that the aftermath for the victim of a crime was often more traumatizing than the actual crime itself. It had taken weeks until her mother had been able to sleep without the lights on. She had to get control of the fear running through her. Had to keep holding on to the fact that God knew exactly what had happened, and even what was going to happen.

"Scoot on over to the passenger side, and we'll look at the options first."

She nodded. Only one thing was clear. They needed to get somewhere safe.

She opened the door and slid across to the passenger seat. "I can shut down the store for a few days, and we'll go check into a hotel down the coast. Somewhere… anywhere that he can't find us."

Except she wasn't certain there was such a place.

He gripped the steering wheel. "What about my dad's cabin?"

"Your dad?" His suggestion took her by surprise. She hadn't thought of him. There was a good chance that their hacker didn't know about Jason's father. The rustic, seaside house was isolated and, knowing Eddie Ryan, secure.

Jason turned and caught her gaze. "Let me drive you, Lauryn and your mother up the coast to his cabin. This would give you a chance to be off the radar there. You remember my father. No one messes with Eddie Ryan. You should be safe there for the time being."

"I don't know." As good as the idea sounded, she couldn't think. The scenarios were back again, swimming through her mind, and none of them came with a good ending.

"Danielle, I understand that you aren't safe here, but this would be much better than a hotel."

She closed her eyes. Eddie Ryan was a six-foot-three, two-hundred-and-fifty pound private investigator who'd spent his life working divorce cases and surveillance, and was a fisherman in his free time. He'd been the one in charge of the family barbecue on the Fourth of July and always one of the first ones to take the Polar Bear Plunge in the frigid Pacific Ocean every New Year. It seemed funny, the things that popped into her mind even though she hadn't seen him for over a decade. Like the time he'd told her she'd broken his heart as much as his son's when he found out he wasn't going to have her for a daughter-in-law.

She pushed away the memories.

"We need to regroup, Danielle. And as sorry as I am, clearly our message didn't work. I'll call in Philip. We'll work together on another strategy. We can also let the police know where we are, but we can't rely on them for our only protection."

Danielle grabbed a tissue from the glove box and blew her nose. "How long will that last? He keeps threatening. I keep running. I can't live this way."

But maybe he was right. At least for now. There was more of a chance that he'd track them down in a hotel, which could put her mother and daughter in danger. The police would help, but their resources were limited and they couldn't protect them 24/7. What other option did they really have?

She closed her eyes and nodded. "Okay. Call your father and make sure he doesn't mind us staying with him for a few days."

Jason took twice the amount of time it normally took to drive to his father's cabin, taking every precaution to ensure they weren't being followed—praying at the same time that he'd given Danielle the right advice. Fixing security matters from in front of a computer was one thing. Dealing with issues that could quickly turn into a life-and-death situation were completely different.

Danielle had said little on the thirty-minute drive other than to explain in more detail to her mother what had happened. By the time they drove into the driveway at half past eight, the sun was peeking through the surrounding trees and Lauryn was sound asleep.

Jason carried the little girl up the front steps to the porch. Between his father's security and the two German shepherds posted outside, no one would be able to sneak onto the property without catching someone's attention. Which was exactly why he'd wanted to bring them here.

Inside, his father quickly made room on the couch for Lauryn who started to stir as he set her down. A quick glance around the room showed little had changed since Jason had last visited, except that there were a few more layers of dust and a few more piles of books in every nook and cranny. The description of homey had, over the years, given way to clutter. He'd noticed the changes after his mother died. Little by little the dining room set and living room furniture had become lost in a sea of stuff. But getting his dad to organize the three-bedroom cabin had long become a losing battle.

Danielle didn't seem to notice. "Mr. Ryan, it's been a long time. It's good to see you again."

Jason's dad pulled her into a bear hug. "Don't tell me you're going to call me Mr. Ryan. Eddie has always been fine, especially to my once-to-be daughter-in-law."

"Dad." He'd have a talk with his father once they got the women settled. Bringing up the past wasn't going to help today's situation.

"Sorry." Eddie glanced at his son then back to Danielle. "It's just good to see you. It's been a long time."

"Too long."

"You remember my mother, Maggie."

His dad turned to Danielle's mom. "As beautiful as ever, Mrs. Taylor."

"Like father, like son, the way you both throw out compliments," Danielle's mom said with a blush.

"I only say what I mean, but I'm glad to hear that some of my charm is rubbing off on my son. All I ask is that you excuse the mess. In a bachelor's life, there always seems to be something more interesting to do than cleaning. But the guest room is off-limits to my clutter, due in large part to the eternal hope that my son will pay me a visit. The two of you, along with your beautiful daughter, can stay there. It has a large king-size bed and a separate twin mattress for Lauryn. Given a little more time, I would have had this living room cleared out, as well."

"Please don't worry at all." Danielle's mom set her small bag on the floor beside her. "We're just grateful for your hospitality."

Jason picked up an unopened package off the table. "I know what I'm getting you for Christmas, Dad. You can store three-thousand-plus books on an eReader and clear out half of this mess."

"After hours and hours of stakeouts over the past couple decades, reading became my weakness." He started clearing off the table in the adjoining dining room. "But while I'm all for developments in technology, there is still nothing like holding a real book. It reminds me of a time when life was simpler."

"I couldn't agree more, Eddie." Danielle's mother smiled, the blush back.

Eddie turned to Lauryn who'd just gotten off the couch. "Well, little lady, I have to say that you're just as lovely as your mother. How old are you, twenty? Twenty-one?"

Lauryn laughed. "I'm almost five."

"Well, you're practically all grown up, then, aren't you? And I've got something you might like. I've got dogs. Would you like to check them out after breakfast?"

"What are their names?"

"Charlie and Chase."

"Do they bite?"

"Only robbers." His father nodded toward the kitchen. "For now, though, I thought you all might be hungry. I might not be the world's greatest housekeeper, but I can cook up a mean plate of waffles and bacon."

Danielle's mom rested her hands against her hips. "And I know someone who can help in the cleaning area."

"Why, Mrs. Taylor, you always did know how to make me smile."

"First names, remember…Eddie."

"Maggie, then. Care to help me?"

She smiled brightly. "I'd love to."

"I could use some help from you, pumpkin, as well, if you're not too busy."

Jason watched as the three of them went to the kitchen, with Lauryn still giggling while her hand clung tight to his father's hand. He turned to Danielle who'd been quiet since their arrival. "Did you catch the look on my dad's face?"

"Yes, because it was the same look on my mother's."

"Stranger things have happened, I suppose."

He'd waited a long time for his father to find love again, but the possibility of finding it with Danielle's mom was an interesting twist. He'd have to process the idea when his distraction wasn't standing beside him.

"Feel any better?" he asked.

"A little. Trying to learn how to find peace, not just when life is easy but even in the middle of the worst of things. Giving up control is hard for me."

Jason helped her take off her coat, before hanging it up on a hook by the front door. "I was thinking this morning about Nehemiah in the Old Testament. He didn't ask for the storm to be taken away. Instead, he asked that he be made strong in the midst of the storm."

"I'm just tired of feeling lost and unbalanced. Everything I grasp on to seems to be unsteady. Just like whenever I think I've made progress, I end up taking a huge step backward."

He reached down and tucked a lock of hair behind her ear. "Just remember that he hasn't won. You're safe. Lauryn is safe. And we're going to do everything possible to keep things that way."

"I know."

Knowing she trusted him wasn't something he took lightly.

Danielle gazed up at him with her beautiful brown eyes. "So, what now?"

Momentarily caught off guard, it took him a few seconds to respond. "I'll call Philip to set up another conference call after breakfast." He pulled his cell phone out of his back pocket. "I have a few ideas I want to run across him, and hopefully he'll have come up with something, as well. Our hacker might have called our bluff, but I'm not ready to give up. He's still running scared and still needs what we have—or what he thinks we have."

"And after you speak to Philip?"

"After that," he continued. "I thought you and I might try a long walk along the beach. It's quiet, private and gives one of the most stunning views of the Pacific I've ever seen."

He watched her contemplative expression, not wanting to push her and yet knowing she needed a break from everything that had happened.

Danielle's answer came with a margin of hesitancy. "I don't want to stay holed up forever, but don't you think that's too much of a risk for right now? If he found us out in the open…"

"While I won't put anything past him at this point, I think the risk is minimal. After one too many ex-husbands coming after my father, he purposely moved here. Even the house isn't under his name. While our hacker might be good, even for him it would take a lot of digging for him to connect us to this place. And with the police after him, I don't see him looking for more trouble."

"I'll think about it," she promised.

"Look at it this way, little time away from reality and fresh air might help you regain your equilibrium."

She smiled up at him, and he was hit with the realization that no matter how all this turned out, he wasn't ready for things with her to end.

The dogs barked outside, pulling him back to reality. Jason skirted past Danielle and jerked open the front door. A dozen birds flew out of a bush. The dogs chased after them. A few moments later, they tired of the game, leaving the birds alone to nest somewhere higher, away from their predator.

But for Jason, it was a reality check of how quickly things could change.

"What was it?" She moved on to the porch beside him.

"It was just the dogs chasing away a flock of birds. Nothing to worry about."

He caught the relief in her eyes. Hiding his worry from the woman he was falling for was becoming harder and harder. The sun broke through the clouds over the mist hanging over the distant tree line. All he could do for now was pray he'd made the right decision in bringing her here.

FOURTEEN

Danielle pressed her tennis shoes into the damp sand and tried to let her shoulder muscles relax. She'd taken a risk leaving Lauryn back at the cabin with her mother and Jason's father, which was why her cell phone was tucked in her pocket in case her daughter needed something before she got back. In the meantime, she tried to put some space mentally between herself and the terror of the hacker's threats.

Sometimes, though, it was hard to know how to live out her faith practically. Trust and reliance on someone else had never come easy. She'd started today by donning a pair of worn jeans paired with a pink fleece hoodie to block the chilly wind blowing off the coastal waters and agreeing to get out of the house. At least the brisk wind sending shivers down her spine was proving to be a welcome reminder she was alive and their hacker hadn't won.

She drew in a deep breath and stared out across the churning waters reflecting the subtle orange and yellow of the sunset. Jason had come with her, but had been sensitive enough to give her the space she needed to think. In the turmoil of the past few days, it had been easy to forget that not only was he facing his own loss, but was having to juggle the current situation with his personal responsibilities of running a company.

Jason had walked beside her the past hour, seemingly content to simply be with her without talking much or trying to fix everything. Nor had he brought up the fact that she'd pushed him away. Instead, he seemed sensitive to her mood. Prying just enough to get her to open up, but not enough to drive her away.

She started walking toward the incoming tide while Jason talked on the phone with Philip. They'd spent the morning and most of the afternoon going over different angles with both Philip and the police. It should have given her hope that the pieces of the puzzle were beginning to come together. Instead, she felt a growing frustration that they still weren't making enough progress.

Which was one of the reasons why she knew she needed to get out of the house. She needed time to let her mind clear and refocus away from the constant stress of the situation. Walking parallel to the waves splashing against the rocky outcropping peppering the quiet inlet was proving to be the perfect antidote. Behind her the thick wooded incline, together with the sea spreading out in front of her, was a demonstration of God's wonder and power. And the one thing she was able to cling to right now. Because if she gave in, the fear of being out of control—spiraling around her like a thick web—would completely consume her.

I'm trying to focus on You, Jesus. To let You be my source of strength, but sometimes it's just so hard.

Danielle tugged up the zipper of her jacket. Learning to put her trust in Him wasn't the only difficult thing at the moment. Something else had emerged from the situation. Faced with the possibility of losing everything, she'd been forced to look again at what was really important. Family, faith, her business…and now Jason. How was it that the thought of opening up her heart again made her feel small and vulnerable, yet there was still a lingering desire to explore the possibility of a relationship between them at the same time?

Danielle spotted a sand dollar buried halfway in the sand and pulled it out, then brushed off the sand to retrieve a perfect, bleached shell. Funny how she and Lauryn could search for sand dollars an entire afternoon and never find a perfect one…and now today, when she wasn't even looking, she'd found one.

Like Jason.

She hadn't been looking for love again, either, but Jason's kiss had stirred something within her. And while she also might have pushed him away, part of her knew she was making a mistake in running from a second chance.

She looked back to where Jason stood talking with Philip on the phone, and realized she'd walked farther than she'd intended. He paced back and forth, intent on his conversation. She started away from the shore toward him, then froze.

Less than fifty feet to her left, a man emerged out of the shadows of the tree line. Close enough that she could see him reach his hands inside the pockets of his zipped sweat jacket. Far enough away that she couldn't read his expression.

He stood still, watching her.

Danielle started running toward Jason. Adrenaline propelled her across the wet sand, heart pounding, breathing heavy. What had she been thinking? He knew where she was. Knew where Lauryn was… Danielle tried to push away the fear beginning to consume her again. She glanced at the figure, trying to suck air into her burning lungs. Two more figures emerged out of the tree line behind the first man.

Jason ran toward her. He pulled her against him, his

arms resting protectively around her waist. "It's just a bunch of guys playing Frisbee. You're fine."

The tall one threw a Frisbee toward the two others. They weren't looking at her anymore. Didn't notice she was standing there shaking from fear.

She closed her eyes, embarrassed at her reaction. Was her faith so weak that each new scare seemed to rip away at her spiritual foundation? That wasn't how she wanted to be. She longed for a steady faith that bore the brunt of the storm with grace.

"I thought..." She opened her eyes again and stared out across the sand. "I thought he'd found me."

"Come on. We'll start heading in the direction of the cabin, but it's a clear night, and I thought you might want to see the stars come out."

She looked up at him and nodded, letting him take her hand as they made their way across the sand. Her breathing slowed down; her heart stopped pounding.

"You okay now?"

"I think so."

"Good." He pulled out a brown paper bag from his jacket pocket with his free hand. "I almost forgot, but I bought something for you yesterday."

Danielle stopped to dig through the pile of white paper wrappers filled with salt water taffy, grabbed a licorice one and found herself smiling. "You remembered."

"I was driving through town last night, saw this little shop open and thought of you."

She pulled off the sticky wrapper and popped the soft candy into her mouth. There was nothing quite like the brightly colored sweet. In college, he'd bought her a bag whenever they'd visited the coast.

"What did Philip have to say?" she asked, reaching for a second piece.

"Rae has disappeared, her rent and utilities unpaid. Her family has no idea where she is."

"I don't understand." Gnawing worry returned. "She was a hard worker, and I thought she was happy. What about her boyfriend?"

"The police have talked to him, but he claims he doesn't know where she is. He did call off the wedding, but said it was a mutual decision."

"What do they think happened?"

"No one knows. Some of her clothes are missing along with her purse and some personal articles. For now they are treating it like a missing person case, but with all that has happened I don't think we can dismiss anything at this point."

Jason studied Danielle's expression in the fading daylight. For the past fifteen minutes, they'd walked hand in hand without saying much, but he could tell by her body language she was finally beginning to relax. Which was exactly what he had prayed for.

And tonight had brought with it an extra benefit. With more rainy than clear days along the Oregon Coast, experiencing a cloudless night was something to be enjoyed. In college, they'd sit out trying to see who could name the most constellations. She'd end up winning because he'd always preferred looking at her. Tonight was one of those nights.

She looked up at him. "I'd forgotten how quiet it can be out here except for the constant rumble of the waves. And the stars…they are so incredible."

"Maybe it's been too long since you've stopped and looked up at the stars. You're finally relaxing."

"I am." Even in the growing darkness, he could see the hint of a smile on her face. "It might be the calm before the storm hits again, but I need to enjoy these moments. Look. A shooting star."

He glanced up at where she pointed, missing the phenomena once again. "You always were good at finding more than I did."

She stopped beside a large piece of driftwood, twisted into the shape of a small bench. "I should get back to Lauryn, but I feel like I need to continue our conversation from this morning."

"Okay." He sat down beside her and waited for her to go on.

"You've been right about several things—about us—one mainly being that there are things you deserve to hear." She clasped her hands in front of her and leaned forward, so all he could see was her silhouette against the backdrop of the gray shadows of the water. "I was awake half the night thinking about you and me, our past, and wondering if there was a possibility for us again... given time."

He hadn't expected this confession from her. He'd expected her to say goodbye when this was all over, not leave things open for the possibility of a future together. He started to say something, then stopped, knowing he needed to let her continue at her own pace.

"I know that situations like the one we are in tend to magnify emotions," she continued. "Which means that what I'm feeling...what we're feeling...might not still be there when all this is over."

"And if there is? Something left to salvage?"

"I don't know the answer to that yet." Danielle pulled her knees closer to her chest, then pulled another piece of taffy from the sack he'd set in front of them. "Do you remember Susie Banks?"

"Your best friend from college?"

"Yeah."

"It's been a long time since I thought about her." He smiled fondly. "She always was a riot. Are the two of you still close?"

"We try to see each other once or twice a year. She remarried and moved to California about six years ago." Danielle pulled the taffy into two pieces then popped half of it into her mouth.

"I don't know if you remember, but her parents got divorced right after you proposed to me. It hit me hard. I loved to hang out at their house after school and on weekends when my mom was working. Since my parents had divorced when I was in high school, I knew firsthand how tough it could be. Even supposedly perfect relationships could end." She glanced over at him then looked away. "I remember watching you with Britney Meyers at some student function about that same time. You were laughing…she was flirting."

"Britney flirted with everyone. Most guys didn't take her seriously. I know I didn't."

"I know that now, but at the time it struck me that could be us one day," she confessed.

All the missing pieces of their past relationship started coming together. Jason shook his head. "You thought I'd leave you just like your father had left you. Just like Susie's father had left her mother?"

She told him about finding out about her father's affair, something she'd never shared in detail with him. About how he'd walked out and taken on a second family. That she'd never seen him again. All these years later the rejection still hurt. Which had been why all of Jason's declarations of love and commitment hadn't been enough.

Sadness filled her pretty brown eyes. "I panicked. The closer we got to our wedding date, the more I knew I couldn't go through with it. I was terrified that I'd end up alone like my mother, raising a child alone... I know it sounds crazy, but it was so real to me back then."

"Why didn't you ever talk to me about it?" he asked, his gut churning with emotion.

"I didn't know how."

He studied her expression, wondering if he should broach the question he'd always wanted to ask. "What made things different when you met Quinton?"

"A lot of things, I guess. Over a year passed before we started to date. I'd spent time on my own in Europe and had to grow up. I also spent a lot of time with an Italian couple I met there. They'd been married for over forty years." She sighed. "I finally realized that not everyone was like my father. Couples married and divorced, but there were also those who stayed together, and men who were faithful to their wives."

"Fear is a powerful emotion."

She'd nodded. They'd both been wrapped up in its effects the past few days.

"I realized that I didn't want to miss out on something again because of fear."

He felt the familiar stir of his heart, but wasn't ready to make any assumptions. "What are you saying, Danielle?"

Danielle felt as if she'd stumbled through her confession. She'd never been good at laying her heart out on the line. Which was one of the things she'd failed at all those years ago when they were together. Admitting that to herself had been hard. Admitting it to Jason even harder.

She pressed her hands against the log and searched for the right words. "I've spent the past couple years trying to keep things together, but I'm tired of trying to just survive. Now over the past week, I've realized just how much I've tried to do things on my own without stopping to seek the will of God in the process."

Why was it that facing struggles always brought about the most growth?

"Do you know what you want?"

His question was the same one she'd asked herself over and over at the beach this afternoon.

"I'm still not sure what I think, except that kissing you last night made me want to run away. Now I'm wondering if I should listen to my heart and get to know the man sitting beside me again."

He looked away from her toward the sea without saying anything. Danielle's heart thudded. She needed to read his expression. Needed to know what he was thinking.

"I'm not trying to play games, or toy with your emotions." She waited until he turned back to her, and let the moonlight gave her a glimpse into his reaction. Cautious. Careful. "The past week has been one of the most frightening things I've ever gone through, but nothing compares to finding out that my baby might be in danger.

"Which is why I've spent the day realizing what is truly important. My daughter, family, my faith and maybe…maybe us." She hesitated, feeling as if she'd just laid her heart out on a platter. "I don't know. Maybe I'm not thinking clearly, but on the other hand, what if I'm foolish to find a second chance at love and throw it away just because I'm afraid things might not work."

Jason sat close enough to touch her—close enough to kiss her—but he kept his hands beside him. She was afraid she knew what he was thinking. What would have happened if she'd come to him and told him this on the eve of their wedding? What if they had found a way to work things out between them?

He pulled back. "I don't want you to kiss me because

your emotions are in turmoil. You've been through a lot. Last night you made it pretty clear that you were not interested in exploring a relationship again. I'm not willing to get caught in an emotional saga that leaves my heart broken again." He tightened his jaw. "I once loved you, Danielle—maybe a part of me never completely stopped loving you—but planning to spend the rest of my life with you then losing you…I don't want to go through that again."

"I know."

"And I'm not sure that this is the right time for us to be making decisions. Maybe when this is all over and life gets back to normal…. But the truth is, you were right when you said you'd been through a lot lately. I'm just afraid that emotion is clouding what you're seeing in me."

She felt the sting of his words, yet knew how badly she'd hurt him. She'd walked away with little or no explanation. Maybe that was why he'd done the same thing over the years. Avoiding a serious relationship in fear that he'd get hurt again.

"What if what I'm feeling right now isn't just the fear and frustration I'm encountering?" she countered. "Something tells me that even if this were the first time we'd ever met, I'd want to get to know you. I'd wonder if you were the one I'd been waiting for. I wasn't ready back then, but I do believe we're both older and wiser now."

He moved closer to her this time. Close enough she could see his blue eyes in the moonlight. The slight smile on his lips. "Are you wanting to try again, Danielle?"

"I just don't want to let something pass me by because I'm too afraid."

He leaned forward and brushed his lips against hers. Instead of pulling away like she had last night, she wrapped her arm around his neck and kissed him long and hard, wondering how long had it been since she'd let her heart feel again.

Jason's phone rang, breaking through the intensity of the moment. Realizing he'd forgotten to switch it to vibrate, he pulled it out of his pocket.

"I'm sorry—"

"Go ahead and answer." She pulled away, breathless, and nodded. "It might be important."

He hesitated, then took the call. A moment later, Jason hung up and turned back to her. "It was Philip. He was able to trace the name of the woman Garrett was dating."

The fear was back in her eyes. "Who is it?"

"One of your employees. Kate Stevens."

FIFTEEN

An hour later, Jason sprinted parallel to the shoreline alone, pushing himself despite his fatigued muscles. The dark waters pooled beneath his running shoes, splashing saltwater around his ankles as he made his way back to his father's cabin. Growing up, the two of them had come here often. They'd bring their German shepherds for runs along the beach, or build a bonfire and roast s'mores after twilight. He'd learned to pray here after his mother died. To fervently seek God's will on starting a business while running this same route.

Tonight, though, his thoughts were centered on what he should do about Danielle.

God, I never believed that Danielle and I would ever have another chance at love but now...even with all that's happened between us, I'm not 100 percent sure how to move forward.

Tonight's kiss had been unexpected—just like her reaction. Having their paths cross again after so many years was the last thing he had expected. Maybe his hesitancy was nothing more than a reaction to avoiding getting his heart broken again. He glanced up at the stunning array of stars above him. He'd spent the past few years using Danielle to measure what he wanted in a relationship and even in a wife. Which hadn't been right. But he'd known that with any more encouragement on her part, his heart was going to cave in. Which was exactly what had happened tonight.

And truthfully, this time it was different. The years that had passed between them had given her confidence and direction. They weren't two college kids unprepared for the realities of the real world.

On top of that, he adored Lauryn. She'd reminded him of his dreams to have a family. Without kids of his own, he'd turned to his sister's children. But while he loved his nieces and nephews, even they couldn't completely take the place of having his own children.

Small bonfires dotted the shoreline, like lights beckoning him to safety. Dealing with Garrett's death and the ensuing fallout from the situation had contributed to his doubts about the future of a relationship with Danielle. But even if they survived the emotional tsunami they'd been swept into, building a relationship meant first taking the time to deal with their past.

Jason skirted around a long piece of driftwood and headed back toward the cabin. Part of him felt as if he were jumping off the edge into the unknown. Relationships had always left him looking for a way of escape. But somehow, Danielle made him look differently at the possibility of losing his heart and falling in love. Because for the first time in as long as he could remember, he was beginning to wonder what it would feel like to stop running.

The familiar twinges of fear that had haunted Danielle throughout the night had begun to fade with the first light of day. The police had put out a BOLO on Kate in hopes of finding her and bringing her in for questioning. But for Danielle, feelings of betrayal had managed to rival her fears over her future. Kate had always been more than simply an employee. They'd been friends. Or so Danielle had thought. Instead, the person Danielle had put her trust in had been living two lives. One, acting the part of a friend. The other lost in some dark world Danielle couldn't even begin to understand.

Danielle snuggled beneath a colorful homemade afghan with a thick mug of coffee between her hands on Eddie's couch, content for the moment to find peace knowing her family was safe. While Eddie showed Lauryn and her mother his stash of spy equipment, her mother attacked the dusty living room furniture with a can of furniture polish and a clean rag.

According to her mother, Eddie Ryan's charm made up for his lack of organization. Danielle, though, wasn't sure what she thought about her mother's newfound romantic interest any more than she was certain where her relationship with Jason was headed.

Which was why she was trying to simply grasp on to the many things to be thankful for—her family's safety, Jason's unwavering support and his father's hospitality. They'd become the beacon in the storm that was making today's situation bearable. For now, she was content to soak up the warm morning sun filtering through the window and listen quietly to the friendly banter between Jason's dad and her mom.

"What do you think, Danielle?" Eddie's question broke into her thoughts. "Do you know how long on average a thief will spend in your home?"

Danielle looked up from her coffee and shook her head.

"Eight minutes. Unless they are there after something specific, the only thing they want to do is get in and get out, so their plan is to grab anything of value that they see and run. Period."

"Makes sense."

"Where do you store your valuables?" he asked.

"Are you asking me to give away all my secrets?" Danielle laughed. "Sounds like a trick question to me."

"Touché, but there is a point to my madness." Eddie grabbed a saltshaker from the cluttered hutch behind him. "Lauryn, can you tell me what this is?"

Lauryn looked up from her coloring book. "A saltshaker."

"Are you sure?"

The little girl cocked her head, then nodded.

"It might look like a saltshaker, but it's actually a small safe. Take off the lid and you can see for yourself."

He handed the saltshaker to Lauryn whose eyes widened as she opened the lid and pulled out a wad of bills.

"See what I mean? Sometimes hiding things in plain sight is even better than hiding it away in a safe." He handed her a dollar bill, then put the lid back on and dropped the saltshaker back onto the hutch. "And that is only one of my secrets. Valuables can be hidden in almost anything. After forty-odd years working as a private investigator, I learned a few tricks. Would you like to see something else?"

Lauryn nodded, seemingly as enchanted as her grandmother.

"Check out this." Eddie rummaged again behind him on the cluttered hutch then pulled out a fancy, cone-shaped listening device.

Danielle's mom stopped beside him, hands pressed against her hips, still clutching the cloth and spray can. "You know you're going to have to eventually clean off the hutch so I can dust."

Eddie shook his head and grinned. "Not sure I can trust a woman who gets between me and my spy gadgets.

Though for you I suppose I might be convinced to make an exception. But first…" Eddie put the padded earphone on Lauryn. "What do you hear?"

The four-year-old's smile broadened. "The dogs are barking outside."

"Exactly. You'd be amazed at the things you can hear with this device."

"Giving away all your secrets, Dad?" Jason entered the living room from the hallway, looking rested—and handsome—in jeans, a white T-shirt and an Oregon Ducks sweatshirt.

"Morning, son." Eddie took the headset back from Lauryn. "Finally decided to get up."

"Funny. I've actually been working the past couple hours."

Danielle caught his gaze and felt her heart stir. "Your father has been entertaining us with all his spy gear."

Jason picked up one of the electronic gadgets from the table. "Isn't this stuff illegal, Dad?"

"I've never broken the law, though I'll admit there are always exceptions to every rule." His eyes crinkled with mischief. "And despite the laws, that doesn't mean I can't have some fun on my own time."

"As long as you keep it on the up-and-up."

The buzzer went off in the kitchen, and Danielle's mom nodded at Eddie. "Breakfast is ready. If you can't clear off the hutch, you could at least try starting with all that stuff at the other end of the table, so I can serve breakfast." She gave him a hint of a smile. "Lauryn, why don't you come into the kitchen and help with the plates and silverware. I made a pan of cinnamon rolls. With cream cheese frosting."

"My favorite!" the little girl exclaimed.

Eddie jumped up and quickly moved the piles of books

and newspapers onto the floor. "Smells delicious, and I have a feeling it will taste even better."

Danielle watched the blush creep up her mother's face as she turned toward the kitchen. When was the last time she'd seen her mother flirt with a man?

Eddie followed her across the dining room. "How have we let so many years go by without seeing each other, Maggie?"

"I've been asking myself that same question."

"We could remedy that, you know. How about dinner in town once this is over. I hear that The Crab Shack makes the best crab cakes along the Oregon Coast…."

Eddie's voiced faded away as he followed her mom into the kitchen. Jason picked up the sound amplifier and held it up to his ear.

"Jason!"

"What?" He shot Danielle a grin then set the gadget back down. "I don't know about you, but I was just wondering if I heard right? Our parents are actually talking about going out on a date?"

"Yes, you heard right. I think it's sweet."

"It's just new for me to see my father so…so smitten over a woman. On the other hand, maybe she'll get my dad to clean up this place once and for all."

Danielle laughed. "One can hope, I suppose."

"What about you?" He stepped in front of her and tucked a piece of her hair behind her ear. "How are you feeling this morning about Kate?"

"I feel betrayed…deceived…. I keep trying to look back to see if there were any signs. Something I missed. How could Kate have lived two lives without my noticing something was wrong?"

"Honestly, I don't know." He let his hand drop and

grasped her fingers. "But knowing it was her does mean that we are one step closer to finding out the truth."

"Which is why I'm trying to remember to count my blessings."

"Like?" he prodded.

"My daughter and mom are safe. I have friends, like you and your father, who are standing by me."

"So do you have any regrets over what happened between us last night?"

She shook her head and felt an unexpected shyness sweep through her, along with a growing anticipation for what the future held for the two of them when all of this was over. "And you?"

"I don't think either of us should rush into anything, but no…I don't have any regrets, either."

"Why don't the two of you come on to the table and get something to eat."

Danielle pulled away from Jason as her mother placed a hot pan of cinnamon rolls on the table. Eddie and Lauryn were right behind her carrying a stack of plates and forks.

"Can I help with something, Mom?"

"You sit right there, eat some breakfast and keep working with Jason to figure out this mess we're in. Eddie and Lauryn can help me finish dishing up the fruit salad and pour the juice he graciously went out and got this morning. As far as I'm concerned, the sooner all this is over, the sooner life can get back to normal."

Danielle helped Lauryn set out the plates and silverware then began serving up the cinnamon rolls. She looked over at Jason from across the table. "You said you've been working this morning. What have you found out?"

"Philip and I are working through audit logs and other files to see if our system has been compromised."

"Have you found anything?"

"So far we haven't found evidence of any security breaches, but if Garrett was the one accessing the accounts, his activity won't necessarily put up any red flags."

"What about Kate? Is there anything new about her?" she asked.

"I put in a quick call to Detective Rodriguez a few minutes ago. As of this morning, she hadn't arrived back at her apartment and her car was still sitting out front."

Eddie appeared with a bowl of fruit in front of her mom who carried a tray with filled juice glasses. Clearly her mom had decided to put him to work.

Eddie offered a prayer of thanks for the food once they all sat down. "I don't know the details of all that has happened, but if you ask me, if Garrett had been smart and done things the old-fashioned way he might not have gotten in to this kind of trouble."

"What do you mean?" Jason dug into his cinnamon roll.

"You understand more than most people, son. We store our information online and the whole world can see it. Even things we think are hidden have the potential to be hacked by an expert." He shook his head slowly. "Life was easier fifty years ago when you hid your money under the mattress, and secrets were never told for the entire world to see."

Jason's brow rose. "So you think we should all stop using the internet?"

"Hardly. I'd say we're both realistic enough to know that isn't a possibility, but thinking about how we use it as a tool while keeping safe is important. I guess I'm saying that none of this completely surprises me."

"And from what I've learned there aren't any perfect solutions." Jason played with another bite of his cinnamon roll with the end of his fork and turned back to Danielle. "So have you decided if you're coming to the funeral?"

Garrett's funeral had been planned for 10:00 a.m. Leaving her little time now to decide.

Danielle reached over and tousled Lauryn's hair. "I'm just not sure I want to leave Lauryn and my mom."

"You know my father." Jason took a juice glass from the tray. "With all of his security gadgets in place, only a fool would break in and try something."

Danielle's mom chuckled as she sat down beside Eddie. "We definitely got a sampling of them this morning. I don't know about the rest of you, but I would hate to go up against this man in an investigation."

"Well, just believe me when I say this isn't the first time my gadgets could come in handy, my P.I. business aside. Besides the dogs, I've got motion sensors outside, and surveillance cameras… Danielle, if you want to go, go. They'll be fine."

Danielle weighed the pros and cons. If she was gone, she'd worry about Lauryn, but not going would leave her feeling guilty. She felt she owed it to Garrett and his parents to be at the funeral. "What about Philip? Is he coming?"

"Yes. Not only will it give him a chance to pay his respects, but we'd like another chance to go over things in person again. The police have already handed over Garrett's computer to him to see if he can trace any communication Garrett had with our hacker. If there is something to be found, Philip is the one who can find it."

Each step was another step closer to the truth.

She turned to Jason and nodded. "I'll be ready to go within the hour."

SIXTEEN

Jason grabbed Danielle's coat off the couch then headed back outside to the car where she waited for him. The temperature had dropped and the winds were picking up as another storm approached from the west. He could hear Maggie and Lauryn laughing in the kitchen as they cleaned up the breakfast dishes. For a moment, he could almost convince himself he was heading off to lunch with Danielle. Not heading off to his best friend's funeral.

Almost.

His dad was starting up the porch steps after feeding the dogs. Jason stopped at the top of the stairs and held up the coat. "Danielle thought she might need something warmer today."

"Smart move. The weatherman predicted this morning that the temperatures were going to drop into the low forties by this afternoon." He climbed up the rest of the stairs and sat down on the porch chair. "You're good for her you know."

Jason shook his head. "I'd say it's more the other way around."

"It usually is with a good woman."

"Like Maggie?" he asked.

"I've been lonely since your mother died."

"I know."

"And with Maggie…I don't know." His father crossed his legs and leaned back. "There's this spark about her. Something that makes me want to get to know her better. To be with her."

"That's usually how it starts. Besides, I'm pretty sure Maggie feels the same."

Denying his attraction toward Danielle had been impossible. Deciding what to do with those feelings was the question now weighing heavy on him.

Charlie bounded up the steps onto the porch and nudged Eddie's leg.

"I guess it's been so long since I've felt this way, but when you get to my age…" his father began. "I don't know. You start to realize that certain things are rare, and you have to snatch up an opportunity before it disappears."

Jason shot his father a grin. "Are you asking my permission to court Maggie Taylor?"

"Since when do I need your permission to go out with a woman?" His father chuckled then reached down to pet Charlie. "I'm just saying that I'm not as young as I used to be. Life is uncertain, and I don't think I want to let this one get away."

"Fifty-five isn't exactly over the hill."

"My knees would tell you otherwise." His father's smile faded. "But what about you and Danielle? You're not planning to let her get away this time, are you?"

Jason glanced across the yard at the car where Danielle waited for him. The last time he'd talked to his dad about his love life he'd been barely twenty years old. In love with Danielle, and ready to say *I do*.

He shook his head. "I still don't know what the future

holds for us. Too much has happened this week for me to even guess."

"What do you feel right now?"

Jason studied his father's expression. They might have always been close, but that didn't mean he was ready to lay open his heart. Not when he wasn't even sure how he felt. "I once knew that she was the woman I planned to spend the rest of my life with. When she broke things off with me, I was forced to question a lot of things. I guess I'm still questioning things. I don't know what else to do but wait and see what is left once this situation is finally behind us."

"She hurt you once." His father leaned forward, catching Jason's gaze. "It's normal to wonder if that could happen again. To wonder if you should take the chance that maybe this is the person you could actually spend the rest of your life with."

Chase ran into the yard from behind the house. Charlie ran down the steps after him barking.

"Are you talking about me or yourself?" Jason asked.

"Maybe both of us."

"Danielle's waiting for me—"

"I know. Just remember that she's not the same person she was all those years ago. You are both looking at a relationship in a very different way than how you did ten years ago."

"Maybe that's what I'm afraid of. That whatever has happened to us this week is nothing more than an emotional pool we've gotten swept into."

"Maybe, but once this is over, you'll have time to figure that out." Eddie clapped him on the shoulder. "You'd better get a move on, son. And don't worry about Maggie and Lauryn. I'll keep them safe."

"I know you will."

Jason headed toward the car, and the reality of the situation came back full force. There would be a time to continue exploring their feelings, but for today, they had enough to deal with. "And, son?"

Jason stopped on the edge of the lawn and turned back to his father. "Yeah?"

"I know I've said it before, but I'm sorry about Garrett. I know the two of you had been friends for a long time, and that losing him has been hard on you. Things like this are impossible to prepare for."

Jason nodded as he went to join Danielle, praying God would grant him the strength he needed to make it through today.

She shouldn't have come.

Danielle fiddled with one of the hearts on her charm bracelet in the lobby of the church building. Jason stood beside her, his hands in the pockets of his dress pants, his silk paisley tie slightly askew. She should offer to straighten it, but somehow, it didn't seem to matter.

Men and women filed past them into the sanctuary, dressed in varying shades of black and gray. Garrett's casket sat at the front, covered with lilies and carnations. The only thing not dreary about the day was the late-morning sunlight filtering through stained-glass windows casting colored beams of light onto the walls.

But all Danielle could think about was Lauryn's and her mother's safety—and memories of another funeral. Her thoughts shifted. No matter how much time passed, nothing could change the fact that Quinton had been a significant part of her life. Situations like today's funeral brought that loss to the forefront. Reminded her that there are no certainties in life. And it hit home how quickly a life could be taken.

She glanced at her watch again. The sooner the service started, the sooner it would be over, and she could get back to Lauryn. "Are you sure Philip's coming? The service is about to start."

"We've still got a few minutes. I'm a bit surprised he's not here, though. Philip's typically always early." He reached down and laced their fingers together. "Listen, I know that coming wasn't an easy decision for you, but it will mean a lot to Garrett's parents."

"I know." His touch brought with it the extra dose of strength she needed. "I'm just…antsy, I guess."

"Worried about Lauryn." He said it more as a statement than a question.

"That and—" she shot him a weak smile "—funerals tend to dig up old memories."

"I won't even claim to understand what you're feeling, but I know for me, I keep expecting Garrett to walk up these steps. I feel as if he's just played some big, bad joke on us all. I still can't quite convince myself that he's really not coming back."

Jason's thumb slowly rubbed the back of her hand. His loss might be different from hers, but there was a connection of their shared loss in today's events they both had to deal with.

"Sorry I'm late." Philip pushed up his glasses as he strode across the emptying lobby toward them.

"You're fine. They haven't started yet."

Danielle started to follow Jason into the sanctuary, but Philip held up his hand.

"I know the funeral is about to start, but before we go in, we need to talk." Philip guided them toward the empty far corner of the lobby and lowered his voice. "I just got off the phone with Lance." He turned to Danielle. "Lance is the only guy I've let in on this to help me."

"What did you find?" Jason asked.

"Here is the thing. As you know, I've spent the past couple days going through both our company files and, more recently, Garrett's files. This morning I found a bunch of encrypted files buried in his laptop."

"Considering Garrett's work, that doesn't sound unusual," Jason noted.

"It's not, but these files were different. All of our data can be encrypted or decrypted by certain passwords. But not these files."

"Why not?" Danielle asked.

"Encryption programs use algorithms and what I found isn't like anything our company has used up to this point. You also need a password to both encrypt and decrypt whatever data you want to ensure is unreadable which I don't have for these files. Long story short, I think I found what our hacker is after. I don't think these guys are after specific intel our company has been protecting."

"Then what are they after?" Danielle bit down on her lip, trying to follow.

"The passwords to decrypt a new security software Garrett was working on. Garrett must have known he'd been compromised."

"Garrett told me he was working on a new program." Jason said.

"Until we get the decryption passwords, I won't be able to know a whole lot more, either, but from what he told me before he died, it's basically a highly sensitive computer program that would help the military and other government agencies track computer activity for viruses and hackers." Philip paused. "Without the password, the information is basically useless. But with the passwords, if it got into the wrong hands, it could be used to undermine our government's security."

Jason shook his head. "If our hacker found out about the program he could try and sell it on the black market. All he would need was a buyer, which for something like this wouldn't be hard to find. The black market for intellectual property is huge."

"Garrett wouldn't just hand someone the software, though."

Philip shrugged at Danielle's statement. "No, but maybe he was somehow blackmailed into giving it to him. Maybe Garrett fed him just the encrypted data until he could figure out what to do. Without the password, the software is useless." Danielle felt a new wave of fear sweep over her. Which was why their hacker was desperate to get his hands on the information Garrett had.

"Wait a minute." She cleared her throat, trying to make sense of what Philip was telling them. "So even if we find Garrett's passwords, we can't give them away. Which means we don't have anything to trade now."

Jason squeezed her hand. "We knew all along that the information Garrett had might pose a security threat if leaked. It's always possible to switch the information we give him."

But Danielle could only think of one thing. With nothing to trade they lost their leverage to get her life back together.

Someone walked through the lobby toward the back of the sanctuary. Danielle turned, momentarily distracted.

Kate?

Danielle blinked her eyes. She had to be imagining things. But there was no doubt the woman slipping into the sanctuary side door was her employee. Familiar profile, curly, dark shoulder-length hair and the purple scarf she'd bought at a local craft fair around her neck.

Danielle felt her breath catch. If Kate had scammed

Garrett, what reason would she have had to show up at his funeral? She jutted her chin toward the sanctuary doors as the young woman walked through them. "It's Kate. She's here."

Jason's brow lowered. "Why would she be at Garrett's funeral?"

"I don't know, but I've got to talk to find her."

Danielle hesitated in the doorway of the sanctuary. The service had started. Music was playing. Someone began singing. Kate turned around. Panic filled her expression as she recognized Danielle.

She squeezed Jason's hand. "I'm going after her."

"Philip, call the police. I'll go with Danielle."

Danielle watched as Kate slipped out of the side door toward the parking lot that was edged by a busy, four-lane road. Outside the sanctuary the wind whipped through Danielle's hooded raincoat as she ran down the steps of the church with Jason right behind her. Kate hurried toward the busy intersection where cars zoomed past, reminding Danielle once again how life didn't slow down for anyone. Quinton was dead. Garrett was dead. Life had to go on.

But not until she found out the truth.

Kate continued down the main street running parallel to the church's property. Where was she going?

Danielle turned back to Jason who was a couple of steps behind her. "Let me try to speak to her alone first."

"Kate?" She shouted above the noise of the morning traffic. "Kate, please…wait."

If she'd heard her, Kate didn't let on. Danielle broke into a run.

"Stop. Please." Danielle grabbed her arm to stop her. "We need to talk."

Kate kept walking. "I can't do this, Danielle."

"You can't do what? Talk to me?"

Danielle caught her gaze. Dark shadows beneath her eyes. She'd been crying.

"I need you to leave me alone." Kate broke away from her grasp and hurried down the sidewalk. "You don't understand. He'll kill me…just like he killed Garrett."

"Just tell me what happened." Danielle quickened her pace.

"You don't know what you're getting involved in. You should have just given him what he wanted, then all of this would be over."

"Given it to who? What are you involved in, Kate?"

"Ian promised…"

Kate stopped at the edge of a sidewalk, struggling to catch her breath. Cars rushed past. Someone honked, impatient. Danielle looked back at Jason who had stopped a few feet away, close enough to intervene if possible.

The police would be here soon. She needed to keep Kate talking. "You conned Garrett. I know that. What I don't know is what made you do it? Or if you were a part of his murder."

"I told you, you don't understand." Kate pressed her hands against her forehead. "I loved Garrett."

"Loved him?" Danielle took a step forward. "Then how did he end up dead? Don't lie to me, Kate."

"It wasn't what you think…."

"I don't know what to think. I thought you were my friend. But now I find out that you've been living a double life? You keep lying to me when my family is threatened. I need the truth, Kate."

The other woman tugged on the end of her scarf and looked behind her, clearly scared. "The truth is that Ian won't stop until he gets what he was promised."

"Who's Ian?"

A spray of bullets exploded into the air.

Seconds passed in slow motion. Someone screamed. Glass shattered in the car beside them. A car alarm went off. Jason grabbed Danielle and pulled her down onto the grass with him, covering her with his body. Her muscles flinched beneath him as a second round of gunfire discharged around. A black SUV zoomed through the intersection.

Kate dropped to the ground beside them.

"Kate!" Danielle crawled across the pavement to her friend. She wasn't moving. Eyes open, gaze unfocused. Blood pooled beneath her head.

"She's been shot, but I can't tell where…"

Sirens blared in the distance. Danielle felt her chest heave. This wasn't how things were supposed to end… Even with her betrayal, she didn't want Kate dead.

"Kate? Talk to me."

Kate's gaze shifted. "He…"

"You're going to be okay."

"I'm…sorry. So sorry.…"

"Kate?"

"He knows…"

"Knows what?"

"He knows where Lauryn is."

An ambulance stopped beside them. Danielle moved back while the paramedics took over. People scrambled around her like she was standing inside a hornet's nest. Danielle pressed her hands against her ears as tears streamed down her face.

Jason pulled her into his arms. "What did she say?"

"Lauryn." Danielle pulled away and stumbled backward. "He knows where Lauryn is."

SEVENTEEN

He knew where Lauryn was.

Danielle grabbed her cell from her purse and frantically dialed her mother's number, letting the phone ring until the voice message picked up. *This is Maggie Taylor, I'm sorry I'm not available...*

Danielle hung up and tried again. After the third time with no answer, she was fighting to breathe. "My mother's not answering, Jason."

"I couldn't get my father, either." The same worry that had taken hold of her reflected in his eyes. "But I did speak to Detective Rodriguez. He's sending a team to my father's cabin to make sure they are okay. We'll meet them there and give our statements then as to what just happened."

Danielle grasped his sleeve as the paramedics placed Kate onto a stretcher and lifted her into the ambulance. Danielle searched the growing spectator crowd, wondering if he'd returned to the scene of the crime. Like vultures circling around her, he was after them. The Hacker...Swindler...Ian... Whatever name he went by, he wasn't just after Kate. He was after her baby.

"We don't know he's found them." Jason pressed his hands gently against her shoulders and forced her to look up at him. "Take a deep breath and listen to me. There could be a dozen reasons as to why they aren't answering, which means we need to assume they are okay, while taking extra precautions."

"Don't try and pacify me, Jason." She pulled away from him and hurried toward the car. "I've seen first-hand what this man can do, first with Garrett and now with Kate. We were foolish to think that we could some-how outsmart him."

At the car, Danielle conceded by handing him the keys. Even she wouldn't argue with him this time that she was in no condition to drive. But despite the fear circulating through her heart, neither was she ready to give up. This guy wasn't going to win.

God, I need You to take care of my baby. To protect her from whatever evil plans have been laid out.

She slid on her seat belt as Jason pulled out of the driveway of the church. Images of Kate lying on the ground, red blood staining the gray sidewalk, flashed in her mind. How had this happened?

Danielle rubbed her temples, trying to waylay the headache that was coming on. "I don't understand how Kate could be involved in this. I thought I knew her."

"You said she mentioned someone named Ian?"

"Yes." Danielle took a deep breath. Focusing on solving the problem was the distraction she needed at the moment.

"What else did she say?"

"She said…he won't stop. Not until he gets what was promised."

"The information Garrett had?" he asked, stopping at a traffic light.

"I'm assuming. She was shot before she could tell me anything else."

"Philip's phone is programmed into my iPhone. Look under favorites, then push speakerphone. He's going to wonder where we went."

Danielle's hands shook as she picked up the phone and called him. "Philip, this is Danielle. I'm in the car with Jason, and we're headed to his father's cabin."

"What just happened? By the time I got to the street corner, the police had already cordoned off the street."

"Kate was shot in a drive-by shooting."

"Are the two of you okay?"

"A little shaken, but okay," Danielle answered.

"We're headed back to the cabin right now to check on Danielle's mom and daughter," Jason stated, "but in the meantime I need you to do something."

"Anything."

"Kate mentioned the name Ian. I know it's a long shot, but see if you can dig further into her background and find a connection between that name and Kate."

"I'm on it."

Fifteen minutes later, Jason pulled into the long dirt road leading to Eddie's cabin. The gate was open. Danielle scanned the tree line, struck by the eerie silence. Something was missing. It was quiet. Too quiet.

The dogs.

Danielle tried to look deeper in the thick foliage. They should be here. "Where are Charlie and Chase?"

"I don't see them."

The squad car had pulled into the circular gravel drive in front of them and signaled for them to stay in the car.

Danielle started to open the door.

"Danielle, wait." Jason took her hand. "Let them do their job. If Lauryn is in any kind of danger, they know how to deal with it."

Jaw tensed, she watched as Detective Rodriguez ran up the front porch beside his partner. It was the same scene she'd watched on a hundred cop shows. But now it was her family's lives on the line.

Seconds dragged by. Rodriguez kicked open the door. A moment later, he signaled for them to come.

Danielle bolted out of the car, and up the front porch. "Where are they?" She stopped short in the doorway. Lauryn's crayons lay scattered across the dining room floor. "Lauryn? Where is she?"

Jason was right behind her. "Dad? Are you okay?"

Eddie sat in the recliner in the corner of the room while one of the police officers worked to untie the rope knotted around his wrists and ankles.

"Besides the whopping headache, I suppose I'll live."

"Where's Lauryn?" Danielle's worst nightmare was playing out in front of her. She picked up one of the broken crayons. "Where is she... Where is my mother?"

"I'm sorry, Danielle." Eddie managed to stand. "I don't know how he did it, but he got in. He must have subdued the dogs—there wasn't any warning. I tried to be so careful and keep them safe, but he hit me, tied me up and now...they're gone."

Danielle felt her legs collapse beneath her. Jason caught her, wrapped his arm tightly around her waist, then led her to the couch.

The room spun. *This can't be happening. They can't be gone.*

"Danielle?"

She heard Jason's distorted voice, coming from far away. "Danielle?"

"They have to be out there." She tried to get up. "Maybe they just went out for a walk with the dogs. Lauryn loves the dogs. We've got to go find them..."

Her mind struggled to focus. She wasn't making sense, she knew it, but she just couldn't wrap her mind around the fact that something had happened to them. She'd lost Quinton suddenly. One moment he was there, eating French toast with her at the kitchen table. An hour later, they told her there'd been an accident. Everyone had been sorry, but there had been nothing anyone could do.

She couldn't lose Lauryn, as well. And her mother...

Someone brought her a glass of water. She took a sip and felt her stomach churn.

"Mrs. Corbett, are you okay?"

Danielle looked up at the officer crouching in front of her. She didn't know what to say. How could she be okay? Her baby was gone.

"I know this is a shock for you," he continued, "but I need to get as much information as I can so we can find whoever took your daughter. Let's start with Mr. Ryan and what happened here. Then I'm going to need to talk to you about what happened back at the church. Do you understand?"

She nodded.

Detective Rodriguez turned to Jason's father. "Start from the beginning, Mr. Ryan."

"We...we were all at the table talking." Eddie's fingers tapped against the wooden arm of his chair. "Lauryn was coloring. I was trying to impress Maggie with stories of life as a P.I. It all sounds stupid now considering I let some criminal snatch them from my protection in broad daylight." His voice broke. "I'm so...so...sorry."

Jason kept his arm around Danielle, but turned to his father. He knew his father well enough to know that it was going to take a long time for him to get past this. "It wasn't your fault, Dad."

"Your son is right." Detective Rodriguez moved to the chair beside Eddie. "And we're going to do everything we can to get them back, but for now, I need you to go slowly through everything that happened when they were taken. The more we know about what happened and who took them, the better our chances of finding them quickly."

"Okay." Eddie rubbed the back of his head where he'd been hit. "Like I said, we were sitting at the table. I heard one of the dogs yelp, so I went out onto the porch to see what happened. At first I didn't see anything, but then..." He swallowed hard. "He was on the porch. He had a gun. He pointed it at me, told Maggie and Lauryn to come with him or he would shoot us all. He must have hit me with the butt of the gun after that, because the next thing I remember is waking up with my hands tied behind me."

"Can you give us a description of the man?"

"He was...tall...thin..." Eddie shook his head. "It all happened so fast, then he knocked me down."

"Dad, wait a minute." Jason glanced over at the table where his father had left some of his surveillance gadgets. "You've probably got him on tape."

"What do you mean?" The detective followed his father across the room.

"Jason is right. I don't have all these gadgets around my house just for fun. This is what happens when you put husbands in jail for beating their wives. There are always a few crazy ones out there who would like nothing more than to let you pay for taking them down."

"So you are saying you got his photo on a surveillance tape?" the detective asked.

"Yep." His dad sat down at his computer and dumped a pile of papers onto the floor. "I've got the outside of the house, both front and back rigged with video surveillance cameras. They're hidden, though, so most people who come don't even notice they're out there."

Jason's phone rang. "It's Philip. Maybe he's got something for us."

"Okay, I found a connection with the name Kate gave Danielle. She has a half brother named Ian Gallaway."

"What do we know about him?" Jason asked.

"Not much, unfortunately, except for the fact that he is a computer whiz. He seems to have wiped his online trail pretty clean, which makes sense considering his profession. Apparently he goes by a number of different names including DragonRider. He's wanted in a half dozen states for fraud charges. Nothing big time yet, but he's never been caught so far."

"Great. Keep digging. I'll call you when we're done here." Jason hung up, his eyes focused on the monitor. "There he is."

The detective turned to Danielle. "Does he look familiar?"

"No, but he fits the build of the man we saw in the truck who tried to run us off the road, and maybe even the man who broke into my shop." Danielle moved back to the edge of the couch and clasped her hands in front of her. "What about Kate? She's the key here."

Detective Rodriguez shook his head. "She's still unresponsive. The hospital will let us know if anything changes."

A second officer came in from outside. "Found both of your dogs. Looks like they were both injected with some kind of sedative, but I think they are going to be okay."

Jason turned back to Detective Rodriguez as his father headed outside to check on the dogs. "So what do we do now?"

"We wait for him to contact us."

* * *

Danielle checked her phone for an email message like she'd been doing the past two hours. Philip had arrived and helped them set up a sort of command center in Jason's dad's living room, searching for clues, anything the kidnapper might have left behind. So far, though, there had been no demands, no communication. Nothing. Kate was still in surgery, which left them looking for evidence in the dark.

"I don't understand." Danielle sat down and took a sip of the coffee Eddie had made. It was strong. Too strong, but she needed the caffeine. The room had finally stopped spinning, but her mind had yet to stop going over everything that could happen. "If he took them, why not let us know his demands?"

They were missing something. And it all went back to the information. And that they still had no idea where to find the information they were looking for.

Jason grabbed one of the dining room chairs and slid onto it backward, clutching the rails on either side. "He mentioned something on the phone that has nagged at me."

"What is that?" Danielle asked.

"Garrett believed that anything could be hacked given enough time and patience. The last time I talked to him he reminded me that nothing was secure, both online and even his phone."

"What did he mean?" Danielle asked. "That someone was tracking him?"

"He was worried about sending files. He believed they would have been compromised. Dad, you mentioned how Garrett should have done things the old-fashioned way. What if he found another way to get the stuff to me?"

"Like sending it via the post office or FedEx?" Danielle asked.

"Yeah." Philip scooted back from the computer where he had been working. "That's possible. And it would explain why I can't find it on his computer."

"Dad..." Jason crossed the room, stopping at a tall stack of unopened mail in the cluttered corner, still unsorted. What if Garrett sent the information to his father?

"Why would he send something to me?"

"Because snail mail can't be hacked." Jason gathered up the pile of junk mail and dumped it all on the table.

"Jason?"

"When's the last time you went through your junk mail, Dad?"

"Don't ask."

"Is there more?" he demanded.

His dad frowned, then pointed at another stack. "Over there."

Danielle started on the pile in the living room while he tackled the dining room. It was a long shot, but anything was better than sitting around and doing nothing.

A few minutes later, Danielle handed him an envelope. "Jason. I think I've got it."

It was addressed to J. T. Ryan from Garrett Peterson.

"What's inside it?" Philip asked.

Jason ripped open the envelope. "Looks like a key to a post office box and a handwritten letter."

Jason paused before reading the letter. Seeing Garrett's handwriting and signature sent shivers up his spine. It was like receiving something from a ghost.

Jason,
You have to understand that I never meant for things to end this way. I'm trying to make things right,

but if I don't, I'm sending this letter to your father. I don't trust technology and assume that they will eventually search your place for the information I have. I should have told you the truth weeks ago. Should have told you the last time we spoke, but when I realize what I've done... How many people are hurt—my parents, friends, you, even our business—I just couldn't bring myself to tell you. Maybe I really am a coward at heart, but trust me when I say that none of this was ever supposed to happen.

The funny thing is that all of this began when I thought I finally found that one person. That soul mate I've been searching for. She was perfect for me, Jason. You'd think so. Or at least in a different life she would have been. Crazy how what I thought was real turned out to be fake. Including her. Which was another reason why I couldn't bring myself to tell you that your best friend and hacker extraordinaire had been taken in by one of the oldest cons in the book. Love really does make you blind.

And I know what you'd be saying right now if the situation wasn't so serious. You'd remind me that I never had good taste in women. The ironic thing about it is that in spite of everything that has happened, I still somehow believe she really did love me. But none of that really matters anymore.

So here is the bottom line. If something goes wrong today, this post office box will have in it everything you need to take him down. And he needs to be taken down. He saw in me an opportunity to take his career to the next level, and I'm not the only one he's targeting. I found out about Danielle Corbett and tried to warn her. Don't let him win.

Everything you need to turn him over to the au-

*thorities is there, including the password. I'm sure
that Philip's on top of all this and will have already
figured out what the guy wants. I just hope he didn't
cause you all the trouble he caused me. All I know,
though, is that if it can happen to me, it can happen to anyone. I'm meeting him at the pier now to
try and put an end to this.
I'm sorry for everything,
Garrett*

Jason finished reading the letter and sat down next to
Danielle on the couch. "I can't believe he didn't trust me
enough to tell me what was going on."

"None of this was your fault, Jason."

"Maybe not, but still…I don't know whether I should
be furious with him, or compliment him for his clever-
ness in getting the information to me. He lost his life
over a stupid computer program. His life was worth a
whole lot more."

"So, what do we do now?" she asked, desperation
creeping into her voice.

"We contact Ian Gallaway. It's time to make a trade."

EIGHTEEN

Danielle pressed through the congested boardwalk beside Jason, trying to calm the panic roiling inside her. Ian was here somewhere. Mingling in the crowd, waiting for them. He'd finally answered their last text and agreed to meet. Their directions had been simple. They would meet him at the west end of the city's annual Seafood Festival. Garrett's information in exchange for Lauryn and her mother. His response had been just as brief. Come alone. No police. No games.

She stopped at an intersection cordoned off for the festival and scanned the crowd streaming through narrow rows of vendors. Last year, she'd brought Lauryn and her mother. They'd feasted on shrimp, oysters, crabs and steamed clams while listening to live music well past dark despite the dipping temperatures. Today, the smell of butter, garlic and fresh seafood filling the air turned her stomach. And instead of watching local chefs show off their culinary skills to groups of admirers, she followed Jason to the prescribed meeting place and searched the crowd for the hacker.

Philip had managed to dig up a ten-year-old high school yearbook photo on Facebook, verifying that the man who'd taken Lauryn and her mother was Ian Galla-

way. She'd memorized his updated features from the surveillance footage. Late twenties, short dark blond hair,
medium height, thick ring on his right hand....

Danielle glanced at her watch. At the edges of the festival where they stood, the crowds had thinned slightly. If
he was here, they should be able to see him. "He's late."

Jason took her hand. "He'll show up. He wants this exchange as much as we do. Just keep walking."

A man stood beside a booth that was selling tuna barbecue. He looked at her, holding her gaze for several long
seconds before dropping his cigarette onto the sidewalk
and stamping it out.

She'd seen him before.

"Jason... The guy just ahead in the faded leather jacket
and jeans... He was at the post office."

"It's not Ian."

The description didn't fit. He was older, balding, with
a distinctive tattoo on the side of his neck. She looked
back to where he'd been standing. He'd vanished into the
crowd. She started walking again. She had to be imagining things.

A woman bumped into her, knocking Danielle's bag
off her shoulder. She stepped aside to let her pass. The
other woman didn't even seem to notice.

Danielle struggled to focus. Details of the plan played
over and over in her mind. While she'd insisted on making the exchange according to Ian's demands, Detective
Rodriguez had assured her that undercover officers would
be present at the festival watching their every move. She
and Jason had already picked up Garrett's package at the
post office. Officers were poised to step in as soon as the
exchange was made.

If everything went according to plan.

She pressed her lips together. The plan had to work,

because Ian was the only person who knew where Lauryn was.

Someone else jostled against her. Danielle started to move aside, then froze. Something jabbed hard into her back.

She could smell the beer on his breath as he whispered into her ear then noted the faded, black leather jacket he wore. "Don't look back. Tell your friend to keep walking beside you."

"Jason? He wants you to keep walking beside us." She looked to Jason then back down at the man's arm that was wrapped around her waist. "Who are you?"

"A friend of Ian's. There's been a slight change of plans. We're going to the pier, away from the crowded festival. You're going to give me the password, then all of this will be over."

"Where's Ian?"

"Let's just say Ian couldn't make it."

"And my daughter. Where is she? We had a deal. The information for my family."

"Like I told you, there's been a slight change of plans. Now move."

They walked toward the pier. Away from the festival, the crowds had all but vanished.

Danielle tried to take in the details around her. Two old men fished for crabs at the end of the pier. Seagulls cried overhead. A boat bobbed in the water beside the massive pillars of the pier.

He was planning to make his getaway.

The man stopped halfway down the pier. "Give me the bag."

Danielle glanced again at the boat. "Where's my daughter?"

A woman yelled behind her. "Slow down!"

Danielle turned around as a thirty-something woman stepped onto the pier with a half dozen boys ready to fish for crabs.

The kids ran toward them, carrying rope, crab pots and traps down the narrow walkway, forcing them to step back. The man lowered the gun in the commotion. Jason slammed against him with his shoulder, pinning the man's arm against the side of the pier. The gun fell to the ground. Danielle kicked the weapon away as police officers swarmed in around them shouting orders.

"Police! Put your hands above your head."

Danielle stood in the middle of the pier, feeling so numb she couldn't even cry. It was worse than the lingering feeling of the weapon pressed against her back, or the terror of wondering if she was about to be shot.

She watched as one of the officers placed handcuffs on their attacker then led him toward the squad car parked on the shore. "I don't understand. Where's Ian?"

Detective Rodriguez tugged on his gun belt. "We don't know yet. The man we just arrested will be taken into custody for questioning, and hopefully we'll know something soon."

"But what about Lauryn…and my mother?" The panic was back. "Without Ian we'll never find them."

Jason tried to get Danielle to eat some of the leftover fruit salad from breakfast, but after several bites she shoved the bowl across the dining room table. Looking up at him, she saw the same worry and fatigue she felt reflected in his eyes. The past few days had worn them out both physically and emotionally. And just when she thought it was all going to be over, the nightmare had taken an ugly twist. All she had now was a list of unanswered questions—and no idea where Lauryn and her mother were.

She picked up Lauryn's stuffed Eeyore off the chair beside her, numb from the waiting. She'd asked to come here, because she couldn't face being in her empty house without Lauryn, but there were signs of her daughter all over Jason's father's home. Her crayons and favorite fairy coloring book. A pink hair band. The polka-dotted backpack she'd bought her for her birthday.

Signs of her mother's maternal, homey presence was just as obvious. She'd spent the morning cleaning the dining and living rooms, apparently convincing Eddie to start going through some of the piles of magazines and newspapers. Something told Danielle that Eddie Ryan's life was about to change forever. As soon as they found them.

God, I need to find my baby...and my mother. Please bring them back to me....

Danielle pushed back her plate at the knock on the front door. A moment later, Eddie let in Detective Rodriquez. Her heart pounded in her throat. The last time a police officer had knocked on her door, he'd come to tell her that Quinton was dead. If he'd come to deliver bad news...

She started across the room toward the detective. "Please tell me you found them, and that they're okay?"

"I'm sorry, Mrs. Corbett, but there is still no news on your mother and daughter."

Danielle felt Jason wrap a protective arm around her shoulders. She leaned into his embrace and closed her eyes for a moment. "If you haven't found them, then why are you here?"

"I have some news I thought I needed to tell you in person." The detective clasped his hands behind him.

"The reason Ian never responded is because he was found murdered."

Jason's grip tightened around Danielle as she felt her world collapse. If Ian was dead, how were they going to find her family?

"What happened to him?" Jason asked.

"They traced Ian to a hotel near the coast where one of the guests heard gunshots and called 911. He was found shot twice in the head in his room."

"And Lauryn and my mother…?"

"They weren't there, Mrs. Corbett."

"What if whoever killed Ian took them?" Guilt laced Eddie's question as he scrubbed a hand over his face.

"That is a possibility, but from what I've been told, there aren't any signs that they'd ever been there."

"Then where are they?" Wriggling free from Jason's embrace, Danielle collapsed down on the couch and ran her fingers through her hair. She didn't want to picture the scene. Another murder. She needed Ian alive. She needed to know where Lauryn was. "Who met us at the festival?"

"He's just been ID'd as Donavan McNeill."

"Who is he?" Jason asked.

"We don't have a lot on him so far, but he appears to be an Eastern European businessman with connections in just about every kind of illegal trafficking you can imagine, including selling intellectual property on the black market."

"So he was after Garrett's passwords." Danielle tried to process the news. Ian's death shoved them another step further away from finding Lauryn and her mom. "Donavan…is he the one who killed Ian?"

"I can't confirm that either way at this point, but I can tell you that he did have Ian's cell phone on him."

"It makes sense." Jason sat down on the couch beside

her and took her hand. "He goes to confront Ian over the promised password and finds out we have it. If our message came through while Donavan was there, he might have realized he didn't need Ian anymore."

"We also found photos of you and your daughter hanging on a board in the hotel room where Ian was found."

"The photos he sent me as proof that he'd been watching us." Danielle fingered her phone in her pocket. Four days ago, she was worried about what to fix for dinner and the high price of gas. How had things come to this? "What about Kate? She has to know something."

"The latest update from the hospital is that there were some complications during the surgery in removing the bullet. The doctors aren't sure if she's going to make it."

Danielle pressed her hand against her forehead, wishing the pain medicine she'd taken thirty minutes ago would start working. "So you're telling me that my baby and my mother are out there somewhere, but we still have no idea where?"

"We are doing everything we can to find them, ma'am, but it might take some take time."

"What if they don't have time?" Danielle tried to hold back the tears, but she'd had enough of waiting and being patient. "We don't know where they are. We don't know if they have food and water…"

"Wait a minute." Eddie looked up from the dining room table where he'd been sitting. "I might know something they do have."

"What do you mean, Dad?"

"I can't believe I didn't think of this before." Eddie started rummaging through the stuff on top of the hutch. "I was sitting here with Maggie this morning talking about my job like I told you before. She was asking questions about my gadgets, and I was trying to impress her with a few tall tales of life as a P.I."

"Get to the point, Dad…."

"Sorry." Eddie stopped and turned around. "It's not here. One of the small portable tracking devices I showed her is gone. It's no bigger than a thumb drive, but she was sitting right there when Ian busted through the front door. If she managed to slip it into her pocket…"

Danielle finished his sentence. "It's small enough that Ian might not have even noticed what she'd done, and we could track them."

Jason didn't look convinced. "Dad, with all the stuff you have lying in this room, you're expecting me to believe that you can tell something is missing?"

"Yes. It was sitting right here at the table. If she was quick, Ian wouldn't have even noticed."

"So we need to see if we can track the signal." Danielle started praying they weren't simply chasing another false hope. "How does it work?"

"As long as it is on, we can track it in real time. I just need my phone…."

Eddie crossed the room to his recliner and dug through the pile of remotes until he found it. "This tracker works person-to-person, which simply put means it doesn't require my using some operation center to tell me where its location is."

"Then how do you find it?"

"The system links to a Google map allowing me to track the location of the device." A moment later he nodded. "It's turned on, and I've got the signal."

Danielle's breath caught. "Where are they?"

"Give me a minute…" Eddie smiled for the first time in a while. "It looks like they're a few miles north of Pacific Cove. There are a few old cabins in the area. The perfect place to keep someone out of sight."

Sitting beside Jason, Danielle's heart pounded as he sped down the winding coastal road flanked by thick foliage and stately evergreens. The men they were dealing with had proven to be ruthless. Which meant while Eddie might have found the location on the GPS, there were still no guarantees that her mother and Lauryn were still there. Or that they were okay.

The Lord is my shepherd; I shall not want...

Danielle pushed aside the negative thoughts and tried to cling to the verse she'd learned as a small child.

Though I walk through the valley of the shadow of death, I will fear no evil.

Sometimes *not fearing* was just so hard to do.

Jason reached across the console and laced their fingers together. "We're going to find them, Danielle."

She squeezed his hand and nodded, choosing to hold on to the hope they'd been offered in the form of one of Eddie's electronic gadgets. Jason was right. Lauryn and her mother had to be there.

Please Lord, let them be okay. I need them to be okay.

"We're almost there." Eddie spoke up from the backseat. "Another...hundred yards and we should see the house."

The run-down cabin sat a mile inland from the coast, with paint chipped off the outside walls, and a front porch that needed replacing. As soon as Jason stopped the car, Danielle jumped out of the passenger seat, ignoring the police officer's words of caution from behind her.

A minute later, one of the officers had broken down the door that had been padlocked from the outside. Danielle stepped into the dusty room, pausing only to allow her eyes a moment to adjust to the darkened room.

"Mama?"

Danielle heard her daughter's voice from the other side of the room. "Lauryn!"

She sat huddled with her grandmother in the corner of the unfurnished room, their hands and feet secured with duct tape. Danielle ran toward her daughter, then pulled her into her arms. Jason and the officer helped undo the tape while Danielle breathed in the lingering smell of cigarette smoke mixed with her daughter's strawberry-scented shampoo.

Her mother stood up slowly, stretching out her cramped muscles. Her clothing was wrinkled, but beyond that, she didn't seem to be hurt.

"Mom." Danielle didn't try to fight the tears. "Are you okay?"

"Besides the fact that we were locked in a house for the past few hours thanks to that no-good man, yes, we're okay."

Her mom pulled the tiny GPS from her pocket and handed it to Eddie with a glimmer of relief in her eyes. "I guess one of your trinkets came in handy, after all."

Eddie wrapped a protective arm around her mother's waist, pulled her toward him then kissed her square on the lips.

Her mother was smiling once he finally let her go. "Why, Eddie Ryan, you certainly know how to make a woman swoon."

Danielle chuckled at the scene, but the reality of what had just taken place—and of what could have happened—wasn't going to be easy to forget. "I'm so sorry you had to go through this. Both of you."

"I'm the one that is sorry." Eddie had yet to move away from her mother. "I was supposed to protect both of you."

Jason shook his head. "There was nothing you could have done to prevent any of this from happening, Dad."

Danielle's mom took Eddie's hand, the relief clear on both of their faces. "It's over. That's all that counts."

"You were smart, grabbing that tracker."

"There wasn't time to think about it, to be honest. What I don't understand is how that man managed to get past the dogs and…"

Danielle smiled up at Jason. Her daughter's chin was nuzzled into her shoulder, and all she could feel was over-whelming relief. "I know there are still lots of unanswered questions, Mom…but for now, let's go home."

NINETEEN

Danielle stopped outside Kate's hospital room and paused before going in. She'd been betrayed by someone she'd always considered to be a friend. Over the past forty-eight hours, details behind Kate's involvement in the case had emerged. In return for a lesser sentence, she'd given the police a full confession, helping to implicate Donavan McNeill. But Danielle still needed answers, and not just from a police report or the ten o'clock news. She needed to hear the truth from Kate.

Jason's hand pressed gently against the small of Danielle's back. "Are you sure you're ready to do this?"

Danielle glanced back at Lauryn, who sat between her mom and Eddie in the hallway, and she couldn't help but smile at the sound of her daughter's laughter. Her family was safe, but there was still one more thing she needed for closure.

"No, but I need to do this."

Danielle sent up a prayer for strength, then entered the room. Kate's hair had been pulled back from her face exposing a long purple bruise across her cheekbone from where she'd fallen. According to the doctors, she'd been lucky. The bullet had hit her shoulder during the drive-by. Farther to the right, the bullet could have struck her heart, and Kate would be dead.

Danielle moved toward the side of the bed, wondering where to start.

Kate's gaze shifted away from Danielle to the blank wall at the far end of the bed. "I didn't think you'd come."

"I needed to see you for myself. To try and to understand what happened. I…I thought we were friends."

"We were." Kate looked at Danielle and caught her gaze. "There were some things about my life that were real."

"Like how you loved Garrett? Or how you put my daughter's life in danger?" Danielle sat down on the edge of the plastic chair beside the bed. "Friends aren't supposed to betray each other."

"What do you want me to say?" Kate's fingers played with the hem of the sheet. "Ian and Garrett are dead, and I'm going to prison. I didn't exactly plan on things turning out this way. What about Lauryn?"

Danielle bit back the anger. "We found her. She's going to be okay."

"I swear I never thought he'd do anything to her."

"From what I know, I don't see how you could have expected it to turn out any different." She glared at the other woman. "You helped steal my identity, tried to ruin me financially, didn't try to do anything when you knew my daughter's life was in danger…and that doesn't even begin to explain Garrett's death. Did you know he had a sister and a niece and a nephew? He was close to his parents. Their lives will never be the same again."

Kate turned away, but Danielle wasn't finished. "The police told me you confessed. The least you can do is tell me why you did what you did."

Kate let out a slow breath. "Ian was family. We grew up together. He's the one who taught me how to live two lives. Showed me how online I could become anyone I wanted to be."

Danielle gripped the handle of her bag and waited for Kate to continue.

"From the beginning, Ian…he promised no one would get hurt. I suppose I never should have believed him, but I loved the adrenaline rush of running a con. And it was easier to believe that it was the insurance or the banks that always took the fall."

Danielle struggled to understand her motivation, realizing how little she knew about the person sitting in the bed beside her. "Why take the risk to begin with?"

"You don't get it, do you?"

"Get what?" she asked through narrowed eyes.

"You're the one who had everything."

Danielle shook her head. "What do you mean?"

"You were the one with the supportive family, trips to Europe, the rich boyfriend who married you and now the thriving business. I, on the other hand, had my grandmother as family, and couldn't even find a job after graduation. You hired me because you felt sorry for me."

"That's not true. I didn't hire you because I felt sorry for you." Danielle's mind spun. So many secrets. So many lies. How could she have missed what Kate felt? "We were friends. I needed help at the store, and you needed a job. Hiring you was an easy decision, and one I always thought you were happy about. Was all of that a lie, too?"

Snippets Kate had told Danielle over the years began to resurface. Raised by an alcoholic mother, then later by her grandmother, Kate had grown up in one of Portland's lower income neighborhoods. Having a difficult childhood wasn't an excuse, but somehow everything Danielle had done to help had instead pushed her away.

"Ian taught me how to run a romance scam." Kate

pressed down the tape of her IV. "At first, Garrett was just another victim. I played it like any other romance scam. I got to know him online, pretended to be interested in him romantically, eventually started asking for his help financially. I knew what to say to get him to trust me and it worked…until I fell in love with him."

For the first time, Kate smiled. "Garrett was different than anyone I'd ever met. Funny, smart, a bit nerdy. We spent hours chatting over the internet. We had so much in common."

"If you really cared for him, why didn't you just walk away from it all?"

"I didn't know how. By that time, Ian had found out Garrett was writing a security program that could be worth a fortune on the black market. He was tired of the typical online scams and came up with a different plan." There was a long pause. "Instead of simply draining Garrett of his savings, I was supposed to be the distraction. He wanted me to meet him in person and get close enough to get passwords and other sensitive information from his computer."

"Did Ian know about your feelings for Garrett?"

"Not at first. How could I tell him I'd fallen in love with our mark?"

"What about Garrett? Did you ever tell him the truth?"

Kate nodded.

"And he believed you?"

"Not at first. I begged him to believe me. Told him I wanted out. Eventually he promised to help me."

"How?

"By gathering evidence against Ian. But Ian was good at covering his tracks, and I knew he had evidence he could use against me if he needed to. The plan was to use the information as leverage to get him to leave us alone."

There was still one more question Danielle couldn't ignore. "Why target me?"

"Ian suspected something was wrong when I started giving excuses about not being able to get the information he wanted. Targeting you was his way of making me prove I was still loyal to him…so I decided to play along with him until Garrett had collected enough evidence."

Danielle's temples pounded. Could she ever trust a person who'd spent her life conning people?

Kate seemed to sense her doubts. "I wanted out, Danielle. You have to believe me. Jealousy—plus the rush— played a role at the beginning, but part of me wanted freedom from playing these games. I thought I could have that with Garrett."

"Why did Ian kill him?"

"Killing Garrett was an accident. Garrett went to Ian to confront him. I begged him not to, but by this point he believed he'd gathered enough incriminating evidence against Ian to take to the police. Garrett just wanted his confession to secure a conviction, but Ian panicked and shot him."

"And the break-in at the store?"

"That was me." Kate's voice was steady, almost emotionless. "I needed to erase the footage of when Garrett had come to visit me at the store. I didn't want you to connect the two of us together. Not until I figured out what to do. I…I wanted to make things right. I am sorry. For everything."

Danielle stood up and slung the strap of her bag across her shoulder. "Sorry for betraying me, or sorry you got caught?"

Kate's gaze dropped at the question.

Danielle swallowed hard. There was nothing more to be said. "Goodbye, Kate."

Danielle walked out of the hospital room, wondering if she'd ever know whether Kate had told her the complete truth, or if she was simply trying to run another con.

Danielle knelt beside the south tower of the sandcastle in order to secure the tiny red flag, then rocked back on her heels to take another look at their masterpiece. She rested her forearms against her thighs and cocked her head. So maybe it wasn't exactly a masterpiece, but the medieval-styled structure did have a drawbridge, gatehouse wall and four circular turrets. Not bad considering they'd made it from a pile of sand.

She turned to Lauryn who was busy filling the moat with water. "What do you think?"

Lauryn splashed a bucketful of water into the moat and giggled. "It's beautiful, Mommy."

"I agree."

"Just like a little girl I know." Danielle tugged her into her arms, tottered for a moment on the uneven ground, then tumbled backward together onto the sand.

"Do either of you want this last piece of chocolate cake? We can't have any of this food going to waste."

Danielle glanced back at Jason and shook her head. "Dessert is definitely going to someone's waist."

"Very funny."

Danielle turned her attention back to Lauryn while they lay against the damp earth, watching the feathery white clouds pass by, thankful for the sun bathing them beneath its warm rays. The sea began tugging at the western wall of the castle they'd spent the past hour and a half building. Danielle moved to grab her camera from her beach bag still sitting out of reach from the tide, so she could snap a photo before the surf knocked the wall down.

Danielle looked up at Jason who stood over her and

smiled. She let him help her up as Lauryn started running across the sand ahead of them, with her red bucket full of sandcastle toys. Jason's arm tightened around Danielle's waist. For the first time in a long time she felt at peace. Like today's clear sunny skies that had swept in unexpectedly after the week's rain.

"It's been a while since I've heard you laugh," he said.

"It's been a long time since I've really felt like laughing. I don't think everything has sunk in yet, though." She leaned into his shoulder as they started walking. "I can't help but wonder how long it will be before I stop looking behind me. Or before I'll let Lauryn out of my sight for more than a minute."

"She's done amazing for all that has happened to her over the past few days."

Details had continued to emerge slowly over the past couple of days as the police worked to put the final pieces of the puzzle together. As far as Danielle was concerned, God had miraculously intervened in a situation that could have ended much worse. It was going to be a long time before she was able to forget the images of where Lauryn and her mother had been kept. She shuddered, unwilling to let her mind try to imagine what could have happened to both of them.

Jason pulled her closer against him. "You doing okay?"

"Just trying not to think about what could have happened if we hadn't been able to find them. I'm thankful the bank was able to sort out the stolen money from my home equity account, but even more thankful that I have my family back." She turned to look up at him, tiredness reflected in his eyes. "What about you? I'm not the only one who's been through a lot. You lost a close friend and are facing some potentially serious security breaches for your company."

"I spoke on the phone with Garrett's parents again last night. It was good for me to be able to share with them and to just listen. I promised I'd stop by later this week. They would like me to help make the arrangements to clear out Garrett's apartment."

"They've still got a tough road ahead of them. How are they coping?"

"As best they can. They're still working through the shock of his death…and it's going to be a challenge for his mom, in particular, to let go of him. The healing process is going to take time, but they are going to a counselor and are blessed with a good support system with their church."

She understood all too well from her own life what it was like to lose a loved one. Some of it only time could heal. And even then, the hole left by losing someone never completely went away.

"Maybe the fact that Garrett died somewhat of a hero will help. He might not have always done things the way he should have, but he did try to make things right and in the end was able to protect you and the company. Plus, he went out of his way to warn me."

"I think it will make a difference. As for the company, I think we've managed to weather the worst of it. Ensuring Donavan didn't get a hold of the password was crucial." Jason drew her closer against his shoulder. "Like you, I don't want to think about what could have happened if they'd gotten their hands on that information. The damage could have been extensive."

Danielle paused to stare out across the sea. Lauryn had plopped down in the sand and started digging again. The breezy afternoon had just enough sunshine to take the chill off. While the grief of Garrett's death in particular still hung heavy, things could have been so much worse.

All I know how to do, God, is thank You for bringing resolution to this situation. And for bringing Jason into my life again.

"On a more positive note, I understand that my dad and your mother are going out tonight on a date."

She looked up at him. "Dinner and a movie, I believe. Sounds…promising."

She'd had a long talk with her mother last night about Eddie Ryan who had somehow managed to sweep her mother off her feet. She was still surprised at the relationship that had sprung up between them so quickly. And while neither of them knew where things might eventually lead, for Danielle it was enough to see the smile in her mother's eyes.

"I'm sure we'll have plenty to discuss regarding our parents, but there are some other things I've been thinking about." Jason stopped and rested his hands against her shoulders. "About you and me, in particular."

Danielle nudged him with her elbow. "Thinking about what that makes us if our parents decide to tie the knot?"

Jason smiled. "That is an…*interesting* thought, but no, that wasn't what I was thinking about."

"I know." She looked up at his familiar features and felt the growing desire to continue discovering more about him.

"A lot has happened the past few days," he began. "Any regrets now that things have settled down and we're away from the emotion of the situation?"

She smiled back at him. "Are you asking if I regret kissing you?"

He chuckled. "That is part of it."

"No." It only took Danielle a moment to formulate the rest of her answer. "And if you're asking if I regret thinking there was room in my heart for you? No. None at all."

Wind whipped at the waves crashing against a row of rocks at the water's edge, but all she could see was the man standing before her.

"That was what I was hoping to hear. Because I definitely feel the same way." He brushed his thumb across her jawline, his gaze intensifying. "You've helped me overcome any barriers I was holding on to from falling in love again."

"Love?" Danielle felt her heart trip at the statement.

"Yes. I love you, Danielle Corbett."

"I love you, too." Any remaining doubts she still harbored vanished as she caught the emotion in his expression. She reached out and grasped his hand. "But there are some things we are going to have to work through."

"Like?" he asked.

She rested her hands against his chest and felt his heart pounding. "Like the fact you live an hour and a half away, for one."

"So you're not interested in a long-distance relationship?"

She shook her head. Neither was she ready to lose him.

"I might have a solution to that," Jason said. "I found this little beach house up the road for rent."

"When did you have time to go house-hunting?"

"All it took was a few inquiries via the internet."

She arched a brow. "What about your job?"

"I happen to be able to work at home. I'd need to drive into Portland once a week or so, but since I am the boss, I don't see it being much of a problem." He tilted up her chin. "Am I throwing out too much too quickly?"

"No…it's just that I never imagined you and me at this place."

"So what about it, Danielle? Are you willing to give us a second chance?"

"Yes." She smiled and wrapped her arms around his neck, anticipating his kiss. "And I have a feeling that this time around we'll get it right."

EPILOGUE

Danielle breathed in the scent of saltwater mixed with the fragrant hint of roses. Deep purple-and-ivory bouquets had been scattered throughout the outdoor reception area. In the background, Celine Dion sang "Because You Loved Me" while Danielle's mother greeted guests in her simple, white wedding dress beside her new husband.

Her mother had insisted on a quiet wedding at a friend's home that was set atop a bluff that looked down across the ocean. Above them, the soft glow of paper lanterns swung gently in the breeze as the sun began to set against the water, leaving a trail of oranges and yellows across the horizon.

"Can I have another piece of cake, Mommy?" Lauryn tugged on the tea-length skirt of Danielle's purple satin dress and held up her empty plate.

"One more, but that's all." Danielle bent over and straightened the lopsided silver hair bow at the back of her head. "If you go to the cake table, Felicia will help you get another slice."

Danielle smiled as Lauryn skipped across the lawn toward the decorated refreshment table. It had taken weeks after the kidnapping for her to feel comfortable in letting her daughter out of her sight. The prayers and encouragement of friends and family had slowly begun to erase her fears that something horrible was going to happen again, but it hadn't been easy. Seeing firsthand how God could bring good out of evil had helped in the healing process. And in the end, she'd discovered a stronger conviction and renewed reliance in God.

A deeper faith wasn't the only thing that emerged over the past few months. Jason's move to Pacific Cove had allowed them time to spend getting to know each other again, something that had Danielle thinking past a dating relationship with Jason to something more permanent. But while they'd spoken of marriage, they both had decided they needed to take it slow, giving them the time they needed to build a relationship.

Jason grabbed her from behind, wrapped his arms around her waist then nuzzled his chin against her neck. "Have I told you how beautiful you are today?"

She turned around until she was facing him, his arms still wrapped tightly around her. "You clean up pretty nice yourself, Mr. Ryan."

Which was true. He'd picked her up wearing a black tux with gray trim and looking handsome enough to cause a girl to swoon.

He kissed her on the tip of her nose. "Did you enjoy the ceremony?"

She worked to rein in her wandering thoughts. "Yes, though it's going to take a while for me to get completely used to the idea that our parents are married to each other."

"I agree, but it's been a long time since I've seen my dad so happy. It's been a good day."

She nodded, content with his nearness that left her feeling beautiful and protected. Since they'd finished the last toast as the sun began to set against the blue waters of the

Pacific, Danielle hadn't been able to stop thinking of her own wedding dreams. A ceremony on the beach with a bonfire in the background. Simple. Rustic, yet elegant… Love had blossomed into something more than she'd ever expected between them, and for the first time she knew she'd found something worth holding on to.

Eddie's voice rose above the soft murmur of the guests. "If I could get your attention one last time. Today is a special day for Maggie and me, and we are grateful for your presence. But the festivities aren't quite over. I'd like you all to give your attention to my son, Jason, who has something to say before Maggie and I head off on our honeymoon."

There were a few whistles and shouts as Danielle looked to Jason, her brow raised in question.

Jason grasped both Danielle's hands and addressed the guests. "This might be our parents' wedding day, but when I spoke to them a few weeks ago, they felt that it was the perfect time to share some things that have been on my heart.

"I'm still amazed that despite a tragic event with Garrett's death and all that happened last winter, God brought good out of it." He turned back to Danielle. "He brought you back into my life. Something I never in a million years would have imagined possible. And now…I can't imagine life without you."

Danielle felt her breath catch as Jason dropped to his knee in front of her. She pressed the back of her hand against her mouth and tried to control the tears welling in her eyes.

Jason looked back toward the guests. "Lauryn?"

Lauren appeared with a small, black box that she handed to Jason.

"Danielle, finding you again has changed my life. Before I met you, I was lost, but with you in my life, I feel as if I found the one person who can fill that void in my life. You inspire me to be a better person, encourage me to reach further and, most important, challenge me to follow God on a deeper level."

Listening to his words, Danielle didn't even try to stop the flow of tears now sliding down her cheeks.

"Because of this," Jason continued, "I know, without any hesitation, that I want to spend the rest of my life with you." He pulled the diamond engagement ring from the cushioned box. "Danielle Grace Corbett, will you marry me?"

Danielle's smile broadened as Jason slipped the ring on her finger. "Yes…yes, I will marry you."

Lauryn clapped her hands beside them as Jason picked her up with one arm, then pulled Danielle against him with his other arm as the crowd shouted their congratulations. But everything—and everyone—faded around Danielle as she caught the mixture of emotions in their depths…. His love for her. Desire to protect her. Anticipation for the future….

She leaned into his kiss, her heart truly free to love again. She'd discovered firsthand how life could be full of triumphs as well as difficulties, but God, in His infinite grace, had stepped in and given her a second chance at both life…and love.

* * * * *

Dear Reader,

I love stories about ordinary heroines who have to face the impossible. When imperfect people are forced to dig deep within themselves to find the will to conquer. Danielle is this heroine to me. I can't imagine having my identity stolen, and even more frightening, I can't imagine not knowing where my child is.

There are times in our lives when we have to face what seems impossible. The loss of a job, a miscarriage, sickness, the death of someone close to us…. Have you been there? Those are the times when we have to remind ourselves that our identity isn't tied to the securities of this world. This world is only temporary. So as you go about your day-to-day life with its ups and downs, my prayer is that you can hold on to the hope that is found in our Heavenly Father. Be strong and take heart, all you who hope in the Lord! (Psalm 31:24 NIV)

Be blessed,

Lisa Harris

Questions for Discussion

1. While this story is fiction, having your identity stolen in the real world isn't. What are some things you can do to ensure that you keep your identity safe?

2. While you might not ever experience identity theft, has there ever been a time where you were taken advantage of by someone?

3. How did you react to the person who had taken advantage of you?

4. Danielle and Jason had to work through their past before they could start a future. Is there a broken relationship in your past that you have worked out, or one that you need to resolve?

5. What are some ways to help heal a broken relationship?

6. When you are in the middle of a crisis, where is the first place you usually turn? Self, family, God, etc?

7. When is the last time you felt like life was out of control and you had to depend on someone else? How did you respond?

8. Jason and Danielle found themselves in a situation where they had to rely on both God and each other. Do you find it difficult to have to rely on other people? On God? Why or why not?

REQUEST YOUR FREE BOOKS!
2 FREE RIVETING INSPIRATIONAL NOVELS
PLUS 2 FREE MYSTERY GIFTS

Love Inspired
SUSPENSE

YES! Please send me 2 FREE Love Inspired® Suspense novels and my 2 FREE mystery gifts (gifts are worth about $10). After receiving them, if I don't wish to receive any more books, I can return the shipping statement marked "cancel." If I don't cancel, I will receive 4 brand-new novels every month and be billed just $4.74 per book in the U.S. or $5.24 per book in Canada. That's a savings of at least 21% off the cover price. It's quite a bargain! Shipping and handling is just 50¢ per book in the U.S. and 75¢ per book in Canada.* I understand that accepting the 2 free books and gifts places me under no obligation to buy anything. I can always return a shipment and cancel at any time. Even if I never buy another book, the two free books and gifts are mine to keep forever.

123/323 IDN F5AC

Name	(PLEASE PRiNT)	

Address		Apt. #

City	State/Prov.	Zip/Postal Code

Signature (if under 18, a parent or guardian must sign)

Mail to the Harlequin® Reader Service:
IN U.S.A.: P.O. Box 1867, Buffalo, NY 14240-1867
IN CANADA: P.O. Box 609, Fort Erie, Ontario L2A 5X3

**Are you a current subscriber to Love Inspired Suspense books and want to receive the larger-print edition?
Call 1-800-873-8635 or visit www.ReaderService.com.**

* Terms and prices subject to change without notice. Prices do not include applicable taxes. Sales tax applicable in N.Y. Canadian residents will be charged applicable taxes. Offer not valid in Quebec. This offer is limited to one order per household. Not valid for current subscribers to Love Inspired Suspense books. All orders subject to credit approval. Credit or debit balances in a customer's account(s) may be offset by any other outstanding balance owed by or to the customer. Please allow 4 to 6 weeks for delivery. Offer available while quantities last.

Your Privacy—The Harlequin® Reader Service is committed to protecting your privacy. Our Privacy Policy is available online at www.ReaderService.com or upon request from the Harlequin Reader Service.
We make a portion of our mailing list available to reputable third parties that offer products we believe may interest you. If you prefer that we not exchange your name with third parties, or if you wish to clarify or modify your communication preferences, please visit us at www.ReaderService.com/consumerschoice or write to us at Harlequin Reader Service Preference Service, P.O. Box 9062, Buffalo, NY 14269. Include your complete name and address.

LISI3R

The pavement outside the Kansas City airport radiated heat even though the sun had already sunk below the horizon. Tate held his seven-year-old daughter's hand a little tighter and squinted against the dying sunshine to read the signs hanging overhead.

"That's it down there," he said, pointing. "Baggage Claim A."

Lily Farnsworth was the last of six new business owners to arrive, each selected by the Save Our Street Committee of the town of Bygones. As a member of the committee, Tate had been asked to meet her at the airport in Kansas City and transport her to Bygones. With the grand opening just a week away, most of the shop owners had been at work preparing their stores for some time already, but Ms. Farnsworth had delayed until after her sister's wedding, assuring the committee that a florist's shop required less preparation than some retail businesses. Tate hoped she was right.

He still wasn't convinced that this scheme, financed by a mysterious, anonymous donor, would work, but if something didn't revive the financial fortunes of Bygones—and soon— their small town would become just another ghost town on the north central plains.

Isabella stopped before the automatic doors and waited

for him to catch up. They entered the cool building together. A pair of gleaming luggage carousels occupied the open space, both vacant. A few people milled about. Among them was a tall, pretty woman with long blond hair and round tortoiseshell glasses. She was perched atop a veritable mountain of luggage. She wore black ballet slippers and white knit leggings beneath a gossamery blue dress with fluttery sleeves and hems. Her very long hair was parted in the middle and waved about her face and shoulders. He felt the insane urge to look more closely behind the lenses of her glasses, but of course he would not.

He turned away, the better to resist the urge to stare, and scanned the building for anyone who might be his florist.

One by one, the possibilities faded away. Finally Isabella gave him that look that said, "Dad, you're being a goof again." She slipped her little hand into his, and he sighed inwardly. Turning, he walked the few yards to the luggage mountain and swept off his straw cowboy hat.

"Are you Lily Farnsworth?"

To find out if Bygones can turn itself around,
pick up LOVE IN BLOOM
wherever Love Inspired books are sold.

Someone is after Tessa Camry—but only she knows why. Now she must depend on bodyguard Seth Sinclair to keep her safe from her past...and give her a reason to look forward to the future.

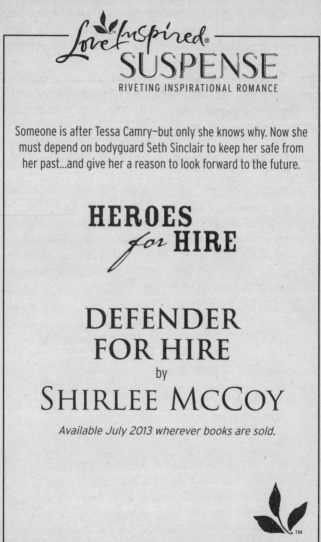

HEROES *for* HIRE

DEFENDER FOR HIRE
by
SHIRLEE MCCOY

Available July 2013 wherever books are sold.